Death of a Maid

Previous Hamish Macbeth Mysteries by M. C. Beaton

M.C. BEATON

Death of a
Maid

A Hamish Macbeth Mystery

NEW YORK   BOSTON

Brea

Mysterious Press
Hachette Book Group USA
1271 Avenue of the Americas
New York, NY 10020

Visit our Web site at www.mysterious press.com.

Mysterious Press is an imprint of Warner Books, Inc. The Mysterious Press name and logo are trademarks of Warner Books, Inc.

Printed in the United States of America
First Edition: February 2007

10 9 8 7 6 5 4 3 2 1

Library of Congress Cataloging-in-Publication Data
   Beaton, M. C.
      Death of a maid / M.C. Beaton.—1st ed.
         p. cm.
Summary: "Scottish policeman Hamish Macbeth is charged with investigating the death of a maid struck down by a bucket of water"—Provided by the publisher.
   ISBN-13: 978-0-89296-010-1
   ISBN-10: 0-89296-010-8
   1. Macbeth, Hamish (Fictitious character)—Fiction. 2. Police—Scotland—Highlands—
Fiction. 3. Highlands (Scotland)—Fiction. 4. Women domestics—Crimes against—Fiction.
I. Title.
   PR6052.E196D4275 2007
   823'.914—dc22   2006018392

7/07
P8°t

For Bengy Wiggin
with love

Death *of a* Maid

Chapter One

I would any day as soon kill a pig as write a letter.

—Alfred, Lord Tennyson

The letter lay on the doormat just inside the kitchen door of the police station in Lochdubh.

Police Constable Hamish Macbeth picked it up and turned it over. From the address on the back, he saw it was from Elspeth Grant. Elspeth worked as a reporter on a Glasgow newspaper, and he had once considered proposing marriage to her but had dithered and left it too late.

He carried the letter into the kitchen and sat down at the table. His cat, Sonsie, stared at him curiously, and his dog, Lugs, put his paw on his master's knee and looked up at him with his odd blue eyes.

"What's she writing to me about?" wondered Hamish aloud. Personal letters were rare and curious things nowadays when most people used e-mails or text messages. He opened it reluctantly. Elspeth always made him feel guilty. She had once jeered at him that he was married to his dog and cat.

"Dear Hamish," he read, "I have a few weeks holiday owing and would like to come back to Lochdubh. As I can now afford it, I shall be staying at the Tommel Castle Hotel. Knowing your vanity, I am sure you will think that I am pursuing you. That is not the case. I am not interested in you or your weird animals any more.

"This letter is just to clear matters up. Yours, Elspeth."

"Now, there wass no need to write such a thing," said Hamish, scratching his fiery hair. "No need at all." The sibilance of his accent showed he was upset. "Herself can chust keep out of my way, and that'll suit me chust fine."

But he was hurt and he felt guilty. He had treated her badly, blowing hot and cold, and the last frost had been caused by the news that his ex-fiancée, Priscilla Halburton-Smythe, was returning to work at the Tommel Castle Hotel, owned by her parents. He could never quite rid himself of the attraction Priscilla held for him. But she had come, seen him infrequently, and then after a month had left again for London. He crumpled up the letter and left it on the table just as someone knocked at the door.

When he opened it, he looked down at the squat figure of Mrs. Mavis Gillespie. Mrs. Gillespie was a charwoman, although in these politically correct days, she was referred to as "my maid." She was considered an amazingly good cleaner. Hamish remembered with a sinking feeling that he had won her services in a church raffle.

She bustled past him into the kitchen and took off her coat. Mrs. Gillespie was a round little woman in her fifties with rigidly permed grey hair, ruddy cheeks, and a long mean mouth. She was carrying a metal bucket and an old-fashioned mop.

Hamish did not like her. "I've decided you don't need to do anything," he said. "The place is clean enough."

"Don't be daft." She glared around. "This place needs a good scrub, and what would Mrs. Wellington say?"

Mrs. Wellington was the formidable wife of the minister.

"All right," said Hamish. "I'll be off for a walk."

"And take your beasties wi' you," she called to his retreating back. "They fair gie me the creeps."

"Women!" muttered Hamish as he strolled along the waterfront, followed by his dog and cat. He knew that the households Mrs. Gillespie worked for probably all had buckets and mops, but she carried her own around with her like weapons. He had once called on Mrs. Wellington when Mrs. Gillespie was cleaning and had winced at the clatter and banging as she slammed her bucket against the furniture and knocked out cables from the back of the television set with her mop.

Why the redoubtable Mrs. Wellington should put up with such behaviour was beyond him. Then he realised that he himself had shown cowardice.

He knew Mrs. Gillespie to be a gossip. Everyone in the north of Scotland gossiped, but Mrs. Gillespie was malicious. If there was anything bad to say about anyone, she would say it. He felt he should go back and order her out, but as he gazed out over the still sea loch to the forest on the other side, a feeling of tranquillity overcame him. He watched seagulls squabbling over the harbour.

Behind him, peat smoke rose lazily from the chimneys of the little whitewashed cottages along the waterfront. Lugs lay across his boots, and Sonsie leaned against his uniformed trouser leg.

The great thing about the peace of Lochdubh, thought Hamish dreamily, was that it acted like a balm on the soul. The guilt and worry about that letter from Elspeth faded away. As for Mrs. Gillespie, let her get on with it. There wasn't much at the police station that she could break.

It was autumn in the Highlands of Scotland, and the rowan trees were heavy with scarlet berries. The locals still planted rowan trees outside their houses to keep the witches and goblins at bay. People said, as they said every year, that the berries were a sign of a hard winter to come, and therefore they occasionally got it right.

Pale sunlight glinted on the water of the loch. A seal surfaced and swam lazily past.

Hamish felt suddenly hungry. He decided to put his animals in the police Land Rover and motor up to the Tommel Castle Hotel to see if he could cadge a sandwich from the kitchen.

Hamish was met in the foyer of the hotel by the manager, Mr. Johnson. "What brings you?" asked Mr. Johnson. "The only murders here now are the fake ones on these murder weekends where everyone gets to play Poirot."

Hamish did not want to say outright that he would like something to eat, so he asked instead for news of Priscilla.

"Still down in London." Mr. Johnson eyed the tall, gangly

figure of the red-haired policeman suspiciously. "I suppose you want a cup of coffee."

"Aye, that would be grand," said Hamish, "and maybe a wee something to go with it."

"Like a dram?"

"Like a sandwich."

"You're a terrible moocher, Hamish, but come into my office and I'll send for something."

Soon Hamish was happily demolishing a plate of ham sandwiches while surreptitiously feeding some of them to his dog and cat.

"Did you come up here for a free feed?" asked the manager.

"I've been driven out of my station," said Hamish. "I won the services of that Gillespie woman in a raffle."

"Oh, my. Couldn't you get rid of her?"

"Too scared," mumbled Hamish through a sandwich.

"The trouble is," said Mr. Johnson, "that nobody wants to go out cleaning these days. Now that the big new supermarkets have opened in Strathbane, they prefer to work there. The staff here has mostly changed. Most of them are from eastern Europe. Mind you, they're good. But those names! All consonants."

"Who does the Gillespie woman work for these days?"

"Let me see, there's old Professor Sander at Braikie. Also in Braikie, Mrs. Fleming and Mrs. Styles, then Mrs. Wellington here, and a Mrs. Barret-Wilkinson at Styre."

Styre was a village to the south of Lochdubh. "I havenae been in Styre in ages," said Hamish.

"Why not? It's on your beat."

"I'm thinking the whole of damned Sutherland is on my beat these days. Besides, there's never any crime in Styre."

"By the way," said the manager, looking slyly at Hamish, "we've a booking for Miss Grant."

Hamish pretended indifference, although he could feel his tranquillity seeping away. "Herself must be earning a fair whack to be staying here," he said.

The Tommel Castle Hotel had once been the private residence of Colonel Halburton-Smythe, but faced with bankruptcy, the colonel had turned his home into a hotel because of Hamish's suggestion, although he still claimed the bright idea had been all his own. The hotel was one of those pseudo-Gothic castles built in the nineteenth century when Queen Victoria had made living in Scotland fashionable.

"Not bothered about her coming up?" asked Mr. Johnson.

"Not a bit," lied Hamish. "I'll be off. Thanks for the sandwiches."

He hung around the village until he saw Mrs. Gillespie leaving. She drove off in her old battered Ford. Filthy smoke was exiting from the exhaust. Hamish stepped out onto the road and held up his hand.

She screeched to a halt and rolled down the window.

"Whit?"

"Your exhaust is filthy. Get to a garage immediately and get it fixed, or I'll have to book you."

By way of reply, she let in the clutch and stamped on the accelerator. Hamish jumped back as she roared off.

Back inside the police station, he looked gloomily around. The kitchen floor was gleaming with water which should have been mopped up. The air stank of disinfectant. Then he looked at the kitchen table. The letter from Elspeth, which he had crumpled up and left there, had gone.

He searched the rubbish bin, but it had been already emptied. He had heard stories that Mrs. Gillespie was a snoop.

He decided to drive over to Braikie, where she lived, on the following day and confront her. He guessed she would protest that it was a crumpled piece of paper and she had just been clearing up, but he thought that he and others had been cowardly long enough.

Then Hamish swore under his breath. He had forgotten to lock the police station office. He went in. The cables had been detached from the computer. He replugged it and then looked around the office, glad that he had at least locked the filing cabinet.

He went back to the kitchen, got out his own mop, and cleaned up the water from the kitchen floor. The work made him relax and count his blessings. With police stations closing down all over the place, he had still managed to survive.

But down in a bar in Strathbane, Detective Chief Inspector Blair was wondering again how he could winkle Hamish Macbeth out of that police station of his and get him moved to the anonymity of Strathbane, where he would just be another copper among many. As he sipped his first double Scotch of the day, Blair dreamed of getting Hamish put on traffic duty.

"I'll have a vodka and tonic," said a hearty voice beside him.

A man had just come up to the bar. Blair squinted sideways and looked at him. He was balding on the front, with the remainder of his grey hair tied back in a ponytail. He had a thin face, black-rimmed glasses, and a small beard. He was dressed in a blue donkey jacket and jeans, but he was wearing a collar and tie.

"Are you from the television station?" asked Blair.

"Aye. Who are you?"

Blair held out a fat mottled hand. "Detective Chief Inspector Blair."

"Pleased to meet you. I'm Phil McTavish, head of documentaries."

Blair thought quickly, the whisky-fuelled cogs of his brain spinning at a great rate. In the past, Hamish Macbeth had always sidestepped promotion, knowing that promotion would mean a transfer to Strathbane. But what if there were to be a flattering documentary about Hamish? The top brass would feel they really had to do something, and he could swear they had a party every time another village police station was closed down, sending more money into their coffers.

"It's funny meeting you like this," said Blair, giving Phil his best oily smile. "I've got a great idea for a documentary."

The following day, Hamish had to postpone his trip to Braikie. He had been summoned by his boss, Superintendent Peter Daviot, to police headquarters for an interview.

The day suited his mood. The brief spell of good weather had changed to a damp drizzle. Wraiths of mist crawled down the flanks of the mountains.

Strathbane had once been a busy fishing port, but new European fishing quotas had destroyed business. Then under a scheme to regenerate the Highlands, new businesses were set up, but drugs had arrived before them and the town became a depressed area of rotting factories, vandalised high-rises, and dangerous, violent youths.

Hamish's spirits were low as he parked in front of police headquarters and made his way up to Daviot's office, where the secretary, Helen, who loathed him, gave him a wintry smile and told him to go in.

Daviot was not alone. There were two other people there: a middle-aged man with a ponytail and a small eager-looking girl.

"Ah, Hamish," said Daviot. "Let me introduce you. This is Mr. Peter McTavish, head of Strathbane Television's documentary programmes."

Hamish shook hands with him and then looked enquiringly at the girl. "And here is one of his researchers, Shona Fraser." Shona, although white, had her hair in dreadlocks. Her small face was dominated by a pair of very large brown eyes. She was dressed in a denim jacket over a faded black T-shirt, jeans ripped at the knee, and a pair of large, clumpy boots.

"Detective Chief Inspector Blair has told Mr. McTavish that your colourful character and exploits would make a very good documentary. Miss Fraser here will go around with you initially to take notes and report back to Mr. McTavish."

Daviot beamed all around, his white hair carefully barbered and his suit a miracle of good tailoring.

Shona looked curiously at the tall policeman. He was

standing very still, his cap under his arm. He seemed to have gone into a trance.

What Hamish was thinking was: I bet that bastard hopes to make me famous so they'll feel obliged to give me a promotion and get me out of Lochdubh. He knew it would be useless to protest.

Instead, he gave himself a little shake, smiled, and said, "Perhaps it might be a good idea if I took Mr. McTavish and Miss Fraser to the pub to discuss this informally."

"Good idea," said Daviot. "Put any hospitality on your expenses."

Once they were settled over their drinks in the pub, Hamish said solemnly, "You've got the wrong man."

"How's that?" asked Phil.

"You see, Blair is a verra modest man. Let me tell you about him." Hamish outlined several famous murder cases which he himself had solved but had let Blair take the credit for. He ended up by saying, "I'm just a local bobby. There's no colour for you there. But Blair! Man, he'll take you to the worst parts of Strathbane. You'll be witnesses to drug raids and violence."

Their eyes gleamed with the excitement of the naïve who have never really been exposed to anything nasty.

When Blair was told later that he was to be the subject of the documentary, rage warred with vanity in his fat breast, but vanity won.

Hamish whistled cheerfully as he drove back to Lochdubh. Mrs. Gillespie could wait until the next morning.

Elspeth Grant was having lunch with Luke Teviot, another reporter. She found Luke attractive. Although a good reporter, he cultivated an easy-going manner. He had thick fair hair and a rather dissipated face. He was very tall.

"So you're off on your holidays," said Luke. "Where?"

"Back to Lochdubh."

"You got a good story out of there last time."

"It's normally the sleepiest, most laid-back place in the world," said Elspeth. "Just what I need."

"I've never been to the Highlands," said Luke.

"What! You're a Scot, a Glaswegian."

"You know how it is, Elspeth. I mean the real Highlands. The furthest I ever get is covering people stranded in Glencoe in the winter. I've never been further north than Perth. When the holidays come along, I head abroad for the sun. I've got holidays owing. Mind if I come with you?"

"You're joking."

"Not a bit of it."

"But why? It's not as if we're an item."

"Don't have to be. I hate taking holidays on my own."

"Never been married?"

"Twice. Didn't work out. Mind you, I was lucky. Both women were rich and were so glad to get rid of me, they didn't want any money."

"Why were they glad to get rid of you?"

"You know what reporting's like, Elspeth. I was hardly ever

home. Come on. Let's go together. It would be fun. I could do with some clean air to fumigate my lungs."

"How many do you smoke?"

"Sixty a day."

"You could stop, stay in Glasgow, and get clean lungs that way."

"Think about it. You could at least have company on that long drive."

Elspeth thought about Hamish. It would be rather pleasant to turn up accompanied by Luke and show him she really didn't care.

"All right," she said. "You're on."

Hamish set out for Braikie the following morning. Braikie was not Hamish's favourite town, although it was miles better than Strathbane, and much smaller. The posher locals referred to it as "the village." It had some fine Victorian villas at the north end, a depressing housing estate of grey houses all looking the same at the south end, and a main street of small dark shops with flats above them stretching out on either side of the town hall and library. A few brave souls lived in bungalows on the shore road facing the Atlantic. They often had to be rescued when November gales sent giant waves crashing into their homes. The main town, however, was huddled several damp fields away, out of the sight and sound of the sea.

Mrs. Gillespie lived in the housing estate. When Hamish called at her home, he noticed to his surprise that she had bought her house. He could see this because she had had picture windows installed, and householders who rented their

homes from the council were not allowed to change the buildings. House prices, even this far north, were rising steeply,
and he wondered how she could have afforded the purchase
price.

Now that he was actually on her doorstep, he could feel his
courage waning. He reminded himself sharply that it was high
time someone put Mrs. Gillespie in her place.

He rang the bell. The door was answered by a little gnome
of a man wearing a cardigan. He had a bald, freckled scalp.
"Mr. Gillespie?" ventured Hamish. He had always assumed
Mrs. Gillespie to be a widow.

"Aye, that's me."

"Is your wife at home?"

"No, she up at the professor's. What's up?"

"Nothing important. I just want a wee word with her. I'll be
off to the professor's."

Professor Sander was retired. He lived in a large Victorian
villa in the better part of town. It was isolated from its neighbours at the end of a cul-de-sac. Hamish could see Mrs. Gillespie's car parked on the road outside. He parked as well and
walked to the garden entrance, which was flanked on one side
by a magnificent rowan tree, weighed down with red berries,
and on the other by an old-fashioned pump.

He was about to walk up the short drive when he stopped.
There had been something he had seen out of the corner of
his eye.

He turned and looked.

Mavis Gillespie lay huddled at the foot of the pump. He
went up to her and bent down and felt for a pulse. There was

none. Her bucket and mop lay beside her. Blood flowed from a wound on her head, and he noticed a stain of blood on the bucket.

He stood up and took out his telephone and called police headquarters. Then he went to his Land Rover and found a pair of latex gloves and put them on. Mrs. Gillespie's handbag was lying beside her on the ground. It looked as if she had been struck down just as she was leaving.

He opened the handbag and looked inside.

The first thing he saw was that crumpled letter from Elspeth. He gingerly took it out and put it in his pocket.

Then he waited for reinforcements to arrive.

Chapter Two

That bucket down, and full of tears am I.

—William Shakespeare

A fussy little man came down the drive. He had a shock of white hair and was dressed in a Harris tweed suit. He was wearing a blue and white polka-dot bow tie. Hamish guessed he was probably in his late seventies. He had a chubby face with a small pursed mouth. He looked like an elderly baby.

"Why are the police here?" he said, then saw the crumpled body on the ground. In death, Mrs. Gillespie seemed much smaller, more a heap of clothes than what had so recently been a living person.

"There appears to have been an accident," said Hamish. "Are you Professor Sander?"

"Yes, yes. How unfortunate. If you want me, I'll be up at the house."

He turned away.

"Wait a minute," said Hamish, "did you see anyone outside your house this morning?"

"No, why? It's not as if it's murder, is it?"

"I'll need to wait and see. There's blood on the bucket. Someone may have hit her over the head. Was she leaving, and when?"

"About half an hour ago. Really, Officer, I don't notice the comings and goings of the home help."

"But you couldn't avoid hearing the comings and goings of Mrs. Gillespie," Hamish pointed out. "She made one hell of a noise."

"I am writing a history of Napoleon's Russian campaign, and when this brain of mine is absorbed in writing, I am not aware of anything else."

"There must already be an awful lot of books about Napoleon in Russia," commented Hamish.

"What would you know about history, young man?"

With relief, Hamish heard the approaching sirens. He was beginning to dislike the professor.

Blair and Detective Jimmy Anderson arrived in the first car. In the second car was the pathologist, Dr. Forsythe. Following that was a people carrier full of the forensic team and in the last car, the small excited figure of Shona Fraser.

"What have we here, Macbeth?" demanded Blair.

"It looks as if someone might have brained her with her bucket," said Hamish.

While the pathologist got out her kit, Blair bent over the body. Then he straightened up, his alcohol-wet eyes gleaming with triumph. "That's where you're wrong, laddie," he said loudly, casting a look in Shona's direction. "There's blood on the stone at the foot o' that auld pump. She must ha' tripped and given her head a sore dunt."

"If you will allow me," said the pathologist. She pushed Blair aside and bent over the body.

There was a long silence while she investigated. The day was dry, but a mist was coming down, turning the landscape into a uniform grey.

A seagull wheeled and screeched overhead. Rowan berries, bright as blood, fell down from the tree.

At last, Dr. Forsythe straightened up. "I can tell you more when I make a proper examination, but, yes, it seems someone struck her a murderous blow on the back of her head with her own bucket. She fell forward and struck her forehead on the stone in front of the pump."

"There might have been a struggle," said Hamish. "You can see where the gravel at the foot of the drive has been all scraped."

Blair rounded on him in a fury. "You," he snarled, "had she any relatives?"

"There's a husband."

"Well, get over there and break the news to him and let the experts get on with their job."

Hamish touched his cap and walked over to his Land Rover. The forensic team were getting kitted out. A strong smell of stale booze emanated from the lot of them. Hamish remembered there had been a rugby match the night before. No doubt they had all been celebrating as usual.

Shona ran after him. "You got it right. He didn't," she said.

"Och, Blair's a bright man. Stick with him," said Hamish hurriedly, and jumped into the Land Rover.

One of the nastiest parts of a policeman's job, reflected Hamish, was breaking the news to the loved ones.

With reluctance, he drove to the housing estate, parked outside the Gillespies' home, and went slowly up the path and rang the bell.

Mr. Gillespie answered the door. "I am afraid I have bad news, sir," said Hamish, removing his cap. "Your wife is dead." He knew from experience that it was kinder to get the brutal truth out fast rather than keep some relative or husband or wife on the doorstep with mumblings of an accident.

"Dead? How? A stroke?"

"May I come in?"

"Aye, come ben."

He stood aside and ushered Hamish into the living room. Hamish's eyes took in the large television set and expensive DVD recorder before he turned to Mr. Gillespie. "Please sit down," Hamish said.

Mr. Gillespie sat down in an armchair on one side of the fire, and Hamish folded his long length into another.

"How did she die?" asked Mr. Gillespie.

"It looks as if someone hit her on the head with that bucket of hers."

Mr. Gillespie raised a trembling hand to his mouth. He took out a clean handkerchief and covered his face. His shoulders shook.

Hamish looked at him in sudden suspicion. "Are you laughing?"

Mr. Gillespie lowered his handkerchief. He laughed and laughed. Grief takes people strange ways, thought Hamish, but Mr. Gillespie's laughter was more merry than hysterical.

"You see," said Mr. Gillespie at last, mopping his eyes, "that bucket was her weapon." He bent forward and tapped his scalp. "Look!" On his freckled scalp Hamish saw an old scar. "Herself did that with her damn bucket."

"You mean you were a battered husband?"

"That's a fact."

"Why didn't you report her?"

"I've got cancer of the stomach. I'm on my second session o' chemo. I can't work. Hers was the only income we had."

"I notice you bought this house. She must have made a fair bit from cleaning," said Hamish.

"That was me. I used to have a good bit of money put by."

"I'll check the estimated time of death," said Hamish, "but I think I'm going to be your alibi. Do you have a car?"

"No."

"I don't see how you could have got over there to kill her. Have you anyone who can come and sit with you?"

"And share my relief? I don't need anyone. I'm going to sit here and get well and truly drunk. And I'm going to watch American wrestling. She'd never let me do that." He hugged his knees. "And I can see my daughter again. Heather's my daughter by my first marriage. Mavis hated her, so she never came around."

"Do you know anyone who might have wanted to kill her?"

"Apart from me? Oh, lots, I should think. She never had a good word to say about anyone."

"Did she have a desk in the house? Any papers or letters I could look at?" Hamish was beginning to wonder whether the snooping cleaner had gone in for blackmail.

"No, nothing. She said paper carried dust. Never allowed a book in the house. Oh, my, now I can sign on at the library."

"There must be bank statements somewhere."

"We'll look if you like. She handled all the bills."

But to Hamish's amazement, after a diligent search, he could not find a bankbook or bill anywhere in the house.

"Where did she bank?" he asked.

"I don't know."

"But, man, when you were working, you must have had a pay cheque."

"I worked over in Strathbane at the men's outfitters, Brown and Simpson. I gave my cheques to Mavis, and she banked them."

"She must have given you money to buy things."

"Mavis gave me a packed lunch and my bus fare. That was all."

"The deeds to the house must be somewhere."

Mr. Gillespie gave a shrug while Hamish stared at him, baffled.

Hamish stood outside the house and wondered what to do next. Then he remembered there was only one bank in Braikie, the Highland and Island. It was a new bank, but surely they would have taken over the accounts of the old one.

He drove to the main street and parked outside the bank.

Inside, he had to wait for the manager. He hoped the manager would not turn out to be one of those men who keep a person waiting to reinforce their own importance.

But a woman appeared from the manager's office, and Hamish was told he could go in.

The manager introduced himself as Mr. Queen. He was a tall, cadaverous highlander, the lines of whose face seemed set in perpetual gloom as if he had perfected the refusal of loans over the years and so the results had become marked on his face.

Hamish explained about the death of Mrs. Gillespie and asked if she had banked with the Highland and Island. Mr. Queen's long bony fingers rattled over the keys of a computer on his desk. "Aye," he said, leaning back and staring at the screen.

"May I see a printout of her account?"

Mr. Queen stared at the tall policeman, his eyes shadowed by heavy, shaggy brows.

"I can get a warrant," said Hamish.

"I suppose you can. I'll print it off."

Hamish waited while the statement rattled out of the printer.

Mr. Queen handed it over. On her death, Mrs. Gillespie had twenty thousand pounds in her checking account.

Hamish raised puzzled eyes. "There were no bankbooks or statements in her house."

"She asked for nothing to be sent to her."

"And these payments as far as I can see, looking back, were all made in cash?"

"Yes."

"Didn't that strike you as odd?"

"I never really studied her account before. She'd pay the money in to one of the tellers. She would have memorised or kept a note of her bank account number and paid the money in with one of the forms on the counter."

"The house, now. She bought her council house."

"That's another search," he said gloomily. "Wait here."

Hamish waited impatiently, his brain whirling. Mrs. Gillespie was a gossip. Mrs. Gillespie had taken that letter from Elspeth. If she could do a thing like that, then she probably snooped on her employers. Everything seemed to point to blackmail.

A seagull landed on the windowsill and stared at Hamish with beady eyes before flying off. The wind was getting up. A discarded newspaper, blown upwards outside, did two entrechats and disappeared up into the darkening sky.

At last, Mr. Queen came back. "Aye, she bought her house twenty years ago when council houses up here were going cheap. At that time, she and her husband had a joint account. They paid for it fair and square. Only cost fifteen thousand pounds at that time. They got a mortgage and paid it off. That would be about ten years ago. Then Mrs. Gillespie cancelled the joint account two years ago. Her husband agreed. It's after that that all the payments were made in cash."

"I'll be off," said Hamish. "You'll no doubt be getting a visit from my superior, Detective Chief Inspector Blair."

Hamish returned to the professor's house. The forensic team were still at work. Blair was in his car with the heater running, swigging something from a flask.

Hamish rapped on the window.

"Whit?" demanded Blair, lowering the window.

Hamish told him about the bank statements and finished by saying, "She could have been blackmailing some of the people she worked for."

Blair stared past Hamish. Hamish turned and saw the diminutive figure of Shona Fraser, who had been listening eagerly to every word.

"Tell Jimmy Anderson what you've got," snapped Blair, "and get back to your police station and await further orders."

Hamish moved away. Shona followed him. She looked up at him suspiciously. "I'm still waiting for signs of the great detective from Mr. Blair."

"Oh, hang in there. He's deep. Verra deep. You wouldnae think it, but the wheels of his brain are turning."

Hamish saw Jimmy and hailed him. He handed Jimmy the bank statements and told him about his suspicions of blackmail.

"You'd better start interviewing them," said Jimmy. "I'll tackle the professor."

"I've been told by the old sod to get back to the police station."

Jimmy took out a list of names. "Tell you what, go over

and see this Mrs. Barret-Wilkinson at Styre, and I'll clear with Blair." His blue eyes in his foxy face narrowed as he saw Shona talking to Blair. "What's the wee lassie doing?"

"Strathbane Television wants to do a documentary on Blair, the great detective. She's a researcher."

"Let's hope she finds some intelligence in that whisky-soaked brain. Talking of which—have you any whisky at that station of yours?"

"About half a bottle."

"That'll do. I'll call on you this evening." Unlike his superior, Detective Inspector Jimmy Anderson had a great respect for Hamish's police work.

Hamish drove back to Lochdubh and collected his pets and put them in the police Land Rover and then took the road to Styre. Styre was more of a hamlet than a village, consisting of only a few fishermen's cottages, three villas, and a small general store.

It lay on the small sea loch of Styre which formed a sort of bay, affording little protection from the might of the Atlantic, lying just outside.

Hamish's stomach gave a rumble, reminding himself he hadn't eaten. He parked in front of the general store, owned, as he remembered, by a Mrs. Beattie. Mrs. Beattie, a small, fussy woman, was behind the counter. The shop was dark, the shelves crowded with very old-looking tins of stuff, sacks of feed, coils of rope, and lobster pots.

"It's Mr. Macbeth!" exclaimed Mrs. Beattie. "You havenae been around here this age."

"I'm looking for something to eat," said Hamish, "and some tins for my dog and cat."

"The dog and cat food's ower to your left. I'll go and make you a sandwich. Spam all right?"

"Spam's fine."

Hamish collected a tin of cat food for Sonsie and a tin of dog food for Lugs. He knew his spoilt pets preferred people food but decided they'd need to rough it for once. If he could be content with a Spam sandwich, then they could put up with commercial pet food.

After a short time, Mrs. Beattie returned and handed him a thick sandwich wrapped in greaseproof paper. Hamish added a bottle of mineral water to his purchases. "How much for the sandwich?"

"Have it from me. What brings you?"

"Mrs. Gillespie, herself what cleaned for Mrs. Barret-Wilkinson, has been found murdered."

"Michty me! Mind you, I thought she was a nasty woman, but Mrs. Barret-Wilkinson swore she was the best cleaner ever. When I had the flu last winter, I got her to clean for me. She nearly gave me a relapse, bang-bang-banging with that bucket of hers and looking into drawers where she had no right to look. Where was she murdered?"

"Outside Professor Sander's place."

"How?"

"It looks as if someone brained her with her bucket. What's Mrs. Barret-Wilkinson like?"

"Verra much the lady. Verra proper. English, of course."

"What's herself doing up here?"

"Quality of life."

"Oh, that. Did she find it?"

"Says she does."

"I'll be off then. Where's her house?"

"It's that big villa, just up on the rise above the village. There's a monkey puzzle tree at the gate."

Hamish went out to the Land Rover and collected two bowls and a can opener from the back. He filled the bowls and let the dog and cat out. They both sniffed the food and then looked up at him with accusing eyes.

"Eat it," ordered Hamish. "Nothing else for you pair until this evening."

He ate his sandwich and drank water and looked out over the sea loch. The wind was beginning to come in great gusts. He finished his sandwich, put the dog and cat back in the car, carried their empty bowls down to the water and rinsed them out, before returning to his vehicle and driving off. The light drizzle was turning to heavy rain.

He drove up to the villa and then up the short curving drive. As well as the tall monkey puzzle at the gate, the garden was crammed with laurel bushes and rhododendrons. The wind was cut off by the high stone wall which surrounded the garden. Rain plopped from the leaves of the bushes.

Hamish rang the bell and waited. The door was answered by a tall woman. She was dressed in a well-tailored tweed suit. The tweed was not new—such as Mrs. Barret-Wilkinson, Hamish guessed, would be too sophisticated to be caught wearing brand-new tweed—and yet the clothes sat oddly on her as if her normal style might be something more towny.

"Mrs. Barret-Wilkinson?"

"Yes. It is I."

He judged her to be somewhere in her middle forties. She had thick brown hair pulled back into a knot, a long nose, and small, intelligent eyes. She looked something like a collie.

Hamish removed his cap. "I am Police Constable Hamish Macbeth. May I come in? I have some bad news."

Most people would have blurted out, Is it my son? My daughter? Or some close relative. But she merely nodded and turned away.

He followed her into a dark hall and then into a large sitting room on the ground floor. It was decorated like a scaled-down version of the drawing room of a stately home. The sofa and chairs were upholstered in striped silk. The curtains at the windows were of heavier silk. Over the fireplace was a portrait of Mrs. Barret-Wilkinson—apparently an oil portrait—but Hamish's sharp eyes registered that it was a photograph, cleverly treated to look like an oil painting. A log fire crackled on the hearth of a marble fireplace.

She sat down and gestured to him to do the same. Her stockings were thick, and her feet were encased in sensible brogues.

"So tell me your bad news," she said calmly. Her voice was English upper class.

"I'm afraid your cleaner, Mrs. Gillespie, has been found murdered."

"Good heavens! That's a blow. Now where am I going to get another maid?"

She surveyed him quietly. Why didn't she ask how Mrs. Gillespie was murdered and where? wondered Hamish.

"Tell me about Mrs. Gillespie," said Hamish. "Was she a threat to anyone? Did anyone dislike her enough to kill her?"

She gave a little laugh. "My dear man, I was not on familiar terms with the home help. I haven't the faintest idea. Might be the husband. It usually is."

"The husband has an alibi. Where were you this morning, between, say, the hours of ten and eleven?"

Her face hardened. "You surely have not the impertinence to think that I would have anything to do with it?"

"I must eliminate everyone from my enquiries."

"Well, I was here."

"Any witnesses?"

"I am a bit isolated from the village. I don't know if anyone saw me."

"Mrs. Gillespie had an unexpectedly large amount of money in her bank account. We feel she may have been indulging in blackmail."

"That's ridiculous. She probably won the lottery."

"The lottery would have meant a cheque. All the money was paid in cash."

"I am beginning to find your insinuations a little bit impertinent. Please leave. If you persist in bothering me, I shall complain about you to your superiors."

Hamish stood up. "I must warn you, this is just a preliminary investigation. You can expect a further visit from a detective."

"See yourself out," she snapped.

*   *   *

Before he left, Hamish peered through the windows of the garage at the side of the house. He saw a powerful BMW. She could have raced over the hills to Braikie in record time with a car like that, waited outside the professor's, and struck the cleaner down as she walked to her car. Hamish asked around the few houses in the village, but no one had seen Mrs. Barret-Wilkinson that morning. He learned that she was often absent for months at a time, and it was assumed she went to London. He wondered about Mrs. Barret-Wilkinson. What was she doing living alone so far from anywhere? And there had been something of the pretend-lady about her.

As he drove back towards Lochdubh, Hamish realised that Mrs. Wellington might know something interesting. She was always refreshingly direct.

Mrs. Wellington was in the manse kitchen, a gloomy relic of Victorian days with the rows of shelves meant for vast dinner services. There were still the old stone sinks.

"I heard about the murder," said Mrs. Wellington. "I'm not surprised."

Hamish sat down at the kitchen table and removed his hat. "Why not?"

"She was such a nosy, bullying woman."

"So why did you keep employing her?"

"I tried to fire her. She went to my husband in tears with some sob story. He told me it was my Christian duty to rehire her."

"How was she nosy?"

"I occasionally caught her looking through drawers. She

swore she had simply been cleaning the ledges inside. She was a great church-goer. One time my husband had just recovered from a nasty cold. He didn't feel up to writing a sermon, and so he delivered an old one. Mrs. Gillespie recognised it and slyly asked me what people would think if they knew. I told her to go ahead and tell everyone, but I would let them all know the source of the nasty gossip. My! I remember I was so furious with her, I asked her if she went in for blackmail. She muttered something and scurried off."

"The kettle's boiling," said Hamish, looking hopefully at the stove.

"I've no time to waste making tea or coffee for you, Hamish."

"Apart from Professor Sander, do you know the other two women she worked for in Braikie, Mrs. Fleming and Mrs. Styles?"

"No, I don't. They probably attend the kirk in Braikie. But I'll tell you who will know—the Currie sisters. They sometimes attend church in Braikie for a bit of amusement."

The fact that the Currie sisters, Nessie and Jessie, twin spinsters of the parish, should find entertainment in church services came as no surprise to Hamish Macbeth. He knew local people who flocked to hear a visiting preacher with all the enthusiasm of teenagers going to a Robbie Williams concert.

Of course, he was not supposed to refer to them as spinsters any more. The police had been issued with a handbook of politically correct phrases. "Spinster" was not allowed, nor, he thought sourly, as he headed for the spinsters' cottage on the waterfront, was "interfering auld busybodies," which was how he frequently damned them.

They were remarkably alike, both having tightly permed grey hair and thick glasses. He could tell them apart because Nessie was the more forceful one and her sister, Jessie, repeated phrases and sentences over again.

Other highlanders may have been alarmed to find a policeman on the doorstep, but it was almost as if the sisters had been expecting him.

"Come in," said Nessie eagerly. "We've been waiting for you."

"Waiting for you," chorused her sister.

"Poor woman. Hit on the head with a bucket like that," said Nessie. Bad news travels fast, thought Hamish.

"Was there a lot of blood?" asked Nessie.

"Blood," intoned Jessie.

"Get the constable a cup of tea," Nessie ordered her sister. Jessie left for the kitchen, grumbling under her breath.

Both sisters were small in size, and their furniture looked to Hamish as if it had come from a large doll's house. He sank down into a small armchair and found his knees were up to his chin.

"I was wondering," began Hamish, "if you could tell me anything about two ladies over in Braikie. Mrs. Gillespie worked for both of them. Mrs. Fleming and Mrs. Styles."

"That would be gossip," said Nessie righteously.

"It is known as helping the police with their enquiries," corrected Hamish.

Nessie was delighted to have official permission to gossip.

"Well," she began, "Mrs. Fiona Fleming is a young widow with two teenage sons."

"Can't be that young. How old are the boys?"

"Sky is thirteen and Bobby, twelve."

"Where did she get a name like Sky?" asked Hamish, momentarily diverted.

"I don't know. Off the telly, most like."

"What age is Mrs. Fleming?"

"About forty, I suppose. That's young these days."

"Does she work?"

"Doesn't have to. Her late husband, Bernie, had a series of DVD rental shops all ower Scotland. She sold them off when he died."

"When did he die?"

"Let me see." Jessie came in stooped over a laden tray. "Jessie, when did Bernie Fleming die?"

"About five years ago, five years ago."

"How did he die?"

"Got drunk and fell down the stairs in his house. Broke his poor neck," said Nessie with ghoulish relish.

Hamish tuned out Jessie's chorus and concentrated on what her sister was saying.

"What sort of woman is Mrs. Fleming?"

"Dainty wee thing. Been seen around with Dr. Renfrew from the hospital. Shocking."

"Why?"

"The man's married."

Hamish took an offered cup of tea from Jessie. "And what about Mrs. Styles?"

"Now, there's a right lady for you. Good church-goer and church worker."

"Married?"

"Married to a retired shoe salesman. He's a bit poorly in health."

When Hamish finally managed to leave the sisters' cottage, his head was buzzing. He longed to go and interview this Mrs. Fleming. Had her husband's death really been an accident? Did Dr. Renfrew's wife know about the affair—if there was an affair? He knew from bitter experience that he had only to take some female out to dinner and the twins put it round the village the next day that he was having an affair.

Chapter Three

3 or 4 families in a country village is the very thing to work on.

—Jane Austen, letter to Anna Austen

Hamish hurried back to the police station, thinking so hard about Mrs. Fleming that he only realised when he sat down in the police station office that he had left his pets in the Land Rover.

He hurried out and released them. "You've eaten," he said. They both stared up at him, and then, with that odd telepathy the dog and the cat seemed to have between them, they both ran up to the fields at the back of the station.

Hamish went back into the office and looked up Jimmy Anderson's mobile phone number. When Jimmy came on the line, Hamish said, "I happen to know one of the women in Braikie that Mrs. Gillespie cleaned for—a Mrs. Fleming. Could you persuade the auld scunner that it might be a good idea if I went to see her?" The good thing about being a highlander, thought Hamish, was that one could tell a white lie without any conscience whatsoever.

"Wait a bit," Jimmy said.

Hamish waited impatiently, hearing voices in the background. Then Jimmy's voice came on the line again. He sounded amused. "Our lord and master says you can go."

"Just like that?"

"Aye. That wee Shona lassie was listening, and Blair wants to be a television star, so he said yes. What have you got? You've heard something."

"Tell you tonight," said Hamish, and rang off.

Nessie Currie had given him a slip of paper with the addresses of both Mrs. Fleming and Mrs. Styles. He noticed that Mrs. Fleming lived very near Professor Sander.

As he drove along the shore road to Braikie, he saw that the heaving Atlantic had turned a dirty grey-black in colour, although the sky above was still blue. "Storm coming," he muttered to himself. "I hope I get back before this road gets flooded."

There was no doubt in his mind that the sea had risen in past years. Now the trim bungalows that stood on the other side of the road were frequently deluged. A great buffet of wind suddenly shook the Land Rover, and he was glad to get into the shelter of the main street and then turn off the road which led to the villas.

Like Professor Sander, Mrs. Fleming lived in a Victorian villa with a short drive.

Here there were no flowers or trees in the garden: simply a

flat expanse of lawn. He pressed the doorbell, which chimed out the strains of "Roamin' in the Gloamin'."

The door was eventually opened by a small woman. Dainty was the word to describe her, thought Hamish. She had a small round face, like a doll's face, with wide blue eyes and a little rosebud of a mouth. Her blonde hair was artfully arranged in glossy curls. She was wearing the sort of Laura Ashley fashion which had been popular in the eighties: a long flowery dress with a square neckline edged in lace.

She looked up at Hamish and put her hand to her throat. "My boys!" she gasped.

"Nothing like that," said Hamish soothingly. "May I come in?"

"Of course." She backed away and allowed him to walk past her into the hall before shutting the door behind him.

"This way." She opened a door off the hall and ushered him into a large living room. Hamish blinked in surprise. Everything seemed to be white: white leather sofa and two white leather armchairs, white coffee table, white curtains at the windows, and white-painted bookshelves. A white china vase held white chrysanthemums. Even the carpet was white.

Mrs. Fleming looked down at a little patch of mud from Hamish's boots and said, "I should have asked you to take off your boots. I never allow my boys to wear footwear in the house."

"I'll take them off now," said Hamish.

"The damage has been done. Sit down." For such a small woman, she had a commanding presence.

Hamish took off his cap and sat down on one of the armchairs, which let out a rude noise like a fart. He found to his irritation that he was blushing. "These leather chairs do make awfy rude noises," he said.

"Really?" She sat down in the armchair opposite him. It did not make a single sound. "Now, why are you here?"

"Mrs. Gillespie has been murdered," he said.

What was flickering through those china-blue eyes of hers? Relief as well as shock?

"But that's terrible," she said. "How? Where?"

"Professor Sander's house. She was found lying at that old water pump at the gate. I believe someone struck her down with her bucket."

"Who did it?"

"We're trying to find out. Where were you this morning, Mrs. Fleming?"

"Surely you don't think . . . Oh, of course. You're just asking everyone who knew her. Let me see, I drove the boys to school and then I came back here."

"Did anyone see you?"

"I don't think so. You can ask Mrs. Samson next door. She watches from her window all day long."

"What did you think of Mrs. Gillespie?"

"A rough diamond. Salt of the earth."

In other words, a walking cliché, thought Hamish cynically. "Were you afraid of her?"

"Of course not. She was just the cleaning woman. She came twice a week."

Hamish's hazel eyes roamed round the room. He noticed

a thin film of dust on the bookshelves. "When was she here last?"

"That would be yesterday morning."

"You've got dusty bookshelves."

"Do I? Well, I left her to get on with it, you know." Her little white hands plucked nervously at her gown. "I had enough of cleaning when my husband was alive."

"Was she blackmailing you?" asked Hamish abruptly.

"No! Why do you ask such a dreadful thing? My life is an open book."

"We think that might be the motive for her death."

"I have nothing to hide."

"Not even your relationship with Dr. Renfrew?"

Her face was suddenly contorted with fury. "Get out!" she screamed. "And you can speak to me through my lawyer in future."

Hamish rose to his feet, and the armchair gave a farewell parp. "I will shortly be replaced by a detective, Mrs. Fleming, and if you refuse to answer questions, you will be taken to Strathbane headquarters for interrogation."

"Out! Out! Out!" she screamed. She picked up the white china vase with white chrysanthemums and hurled it at his head. He dodged it, and the vase hit the wall and shattered.

"I could charge you for assaulting a police officer," said Hamish severely. "I'll be back."

"Bugger off, Arnold Schwarzenegger," she screamed.

Hamish stood outside her gate and thought hard. He could not get over the fact that there had been no incriminating papers or letters in Mrs. Gillespie's home. If she had been blackmailing her clients, surely she would have kept letters or something. But where?

He looked thoughtfully at the villa next door to the right. A lace curtain twitched.

He walked up to the door of the villa. There was no bell. He rapped with the old-fashioned brass ring set into the oak panels and waited. Shuffling feet approached the door on the other side, and then it was swung open.

"Mrs. Samson?" asked Hamish.

"Aye, come ben. You're here about the murder. Wipe your feet."

Mrs. Flora Samson was old and stooped. Pink scalp shone through her wisps of grey hair. Her elderly face was set in wrinkles of discontent. She wore very thick glasses, which magnified her eyes so that they looked like the eyes of an old witch asking the children if they would like some gingerbread.

Her living room was crammed with photos in frames. They seemed to be everywhere. The furniture was Victorian and draped with yellowing lace antimacassars. A stuffed owl on a bamboo table stared out of its glass case with baleful eyes. In another glass case mounted on the wall, a stuffed salmon swam endlessly against a badly painted backdrop of reeds and river. A coal fire was smouldering in the fireplace, occasionally sending out puffs of grey smoke. The room smelled strongly of lavender air freshener, which did not quite cover up the underlying smell of urine and unwashed armpits.

"You've come about the murder. Sit down," said Mrs. Samson.

"How did you hear about it?"

"It was on the telly a quarter of an hour ago. The telly's in the kitchen. I don't often watch it, mind, but I keep it on for the sound." The faint noises of laughter and cheering filtered through from the kitchen. A game show, guessed Hamish.

"I have been interviewing Mrs. Fleming," said Hamish. "I have to establish alibis for this morning for everyone Mrs. Gillespie cleaned for. Did you see Mrs. Fleming go out this morning?"

"Aye, she took her lads to school, then herself came back. Poke the fire, laddie. It's right cold in here."

Hamish picked up a brass poker by the hearth and poked the fire and then backed off as smoke poured up into his face.

"Och," he said crossly, "you need your chimney swept."

"Sit down and mind your own business."

"Did she go out again?" asked Hamish.

Mrs. Samson's face seemed to swim through the layers of smoke. "She might ha' done. I had to go to the you know what. It's up the stairs and man, at my age, it's like climbing Everest. It's the arthuritis. Takes me ages."

"We feel that Mrs. Gillespie might have been a blackmailer," said Hamish.

Mrs. Samson's eyes gleamed with malice. A spurt of flame rose from the smoking fire and shone red on the thick lenses of her glasses. "So she might have killed him, after all."

"Who?"

"Her man, Bernie Fleming. Why would a fit man like that fall down the stairs? He wasn't fond of a dram, either."

Hamish was beginning to hate her, but gossip was invaluable.

"Were they a happy couple?"

"Not a bit of it. I could hear them fighting."

"What? From a villa next door?"

"In their garden in the summer when I was taking the air, I heard them. She screamed that she was sick of cleaning and polishing and that he never took her anywhere. Soon as he was dead, she sold all his stuff, all the furniture, and got all modern put in."

"I noticed the stairs," said Hamish. "They're steep and of polished wood. A man could easily slip."

Mrs. Samson snorted. "In his day they were thick carpet, top to bottom."

"How do you know? Had you been in their house?"

"No, but Mrs. Gillespie told me."

"Did she now? Friendly with her, were you?"

"Herself would drop in now and then for a wee bittie o' a chat. Not many'll spend time with an auld woman."

"Did she say anything to lead you to believe that Mrs. Fleming might have murdered her husband?"

"No, but I have my suspicions."

"Did she talk about her other clients?" Hamish consulted his list. "Professor Sander, Mrs. Styles, Mrs. Wellington, and Mrs. Barret-Wilkinson?"

"Och, just a few wee remarks, like Mrs. Wellington was a slave-driver and Mrs. Styles wasn't as saintly as she liked to make out. Never said anything about the other two."

Hamish suddenly longed to get out of the smoky room. He

got to his feet. "I'll be off, then. I may want another word with you. I think Mrs. Gillespie may have been blackmailing her employers." He turned in the doorway. "Did Mrs. Gillespie have any friends?"

"I think she sometimes talked to Mrs. Queenie Hendry, her what has the bakery in the main street."

Hamish's mobile phone rang as he was leaving the house. It was Jimmy. "Blair says you're to get over to the daughter's. No one's broken the news to her yet."

"What's up with her father? Surely he'll have phoned her by now."

"We've just left Mr. Gillespie. He says it would sound better coming from the police, don't ask me why. Here's her address. The Nest, Shore Road, one of those bungalows. You'd think people like that lived in mansions the way they won't give a street number. How're you doing?"

"Got a lot, but I'll tell you in private this evening. I don't want Blair crashing around at this point."

As Hamish drove along the shore road, the wind screamed and buffeted at his vehicle, and ahead he could see the first waves crashing onto the road. The Nest had a sign in poker-work outside the gate, which swung and creaked in the wind on two thin iron chains. He wondered whether Heather Gillespie would be out at work, if she did work, but as he opened the gate, he saw a slim figure heaving sandbags in front of the door.

"Miss Gillespie?" Hamish suddenly wondered whether Heather Gillespie was married.

She turned around. Her eyes sharpened in alarm when she saw his uniform.

"May we go inside?" asked Hamish, holding on to his cap against the screeching wind. She silently led the way.

Another living room, this one sparsely furnished in assemble-it-yourself table and chairs. Hamish recognised them, having seen them offered in a DIY shop in Inverness. The room was very cold. The fireplace had been sealed off. An unlit two-bar electric heater stood in front of it.

Heather Gillespie was very thin but with a large heavy head covered in a shock of ginger hair. Her eyes were her finest feature, being large and silvery grey. The colour of Elspeth's eyes, thought Hamish, and suddenly wondered whether she had arrived yet.

"I have bad news," said Hamish. "I am afraid Mrs. Gillespie is dead."

"A stroke?" demanded Heather.

"No, I am afraid herself was murdered."

She turned very pale. "Can I get you something?" asked Hamish.

"No, no. It's the shock. How? When? Where is my father?"

"Mrs. Gillespie was murdered this morning outside the home of Professor Sander. Someone struck her down. Your father has been told the sad news. For some reason, he thought the news would sound better coming from the police."

"Dad's not a well man. I can understand that. I'd better go to him."

"Do you know of anyone who would wish your mother harm?"

"Just about everyone."

"Miss Gillespie . . . it is *Miss* Gillespie?"

"It is now. I was married, but after the divorce, I reverted to my maiden name."

"May I sit down for a minute?"

She indicated the table at the window, and both of them sat down. Beyond the window, the sea tumbled and roared with increasing frequency.

Hamish took out his notebook. "What was the name of your ex?"

"Tom Morrison."

"Where can I find him?"

"In Braikie. He runs the local garage."

"Any children?"

"No. Look, what's this got to do with my mother's murder?"

"I wass chust wondering," said Hamish, the sibilance of his accent showing he was becoming nervous, "whether your mother had anything to do with the break-up of your marriage."

A fat tear ran down Heather's cheek, followed by another and another until she was sobbing helplessly. Hamish saw a box of tissues on the coffee table. He fetched it and put it down beside her.

She wiped her eyes and blew her nose. Then she said in a low voice, "Ma told me that Tom was having an affair with Bertha Maclean, the local tart. I challenged him, and he said Ma was a nasty auld liar. I followed him one night and saw him go up the stairs to her flat. That was enough for me, and I filed for divorce. After the divorce, I met Bertha in the street and had a go at her. She said she had breast cancer and a few of the villagers had been helping her out. Tom had called round to fix a few things in the flat for her.

"I asked Tom about it, and he said Bertha at first didn't want anyone to know she had cancer and had sworn the few people helping her to secrecy. I shouted at him that he could have told me. He said he was sick of living with a woman who was so much under her nasty mother's thumb and he could kill the old bitch. He said Ma had told him that I was sick of being married to him. Of course, I denied it, but the damage had been done. I've barely spoken to my mother since."

"But she isn't really your mother, is she?"

"No, but my own mother died when I was three years old, and I got in the way of calling her Ma."

Hamish reflected that Mrs. Gillespie must have been an evil influence, although Tom and Heather certainly did not seem to have trusted each other very much.

"I'd better go and see Dad," said Heather.

"I'll help you with the sandbags first," said Hamish.

She looked at her watch. "It'll be all right now. The tide's on the turn."

Elspeth Grant had unpacked her suitcase and was looking out of the window of the Tommel Castle Hotel down to where the little whitewashed houses of Lochdubh fronted the sea loch. She opened the window and breathed in a great gulp of pine-scented air.

It was great to be back. There was a knock at her door. She opened it. Bessie, one of the maids, stood there, holding clean towels. "Welcome back, Miss Grant," she said. "You'll be up here reporting the murder."

"Murder? What murder?"

"Poor auld Mrs. Gillespie. Someone brained her with her bucket."

Elspeth suppressed a sudden mad desire to laugh. "Who was Mrs. Gillespie?"

"Herself was a cleaner, lived over Braikie way. You'll be seeing Hamish?"

Before Elspeth could reply, Luke Teviot strolled in. "Hullo, sweetheart," he said cheerfully. "What does one do for entertainment around here?"

Bessie's eyes widened. She put the towels in the bathroom and then scurried off to spread the news around that Elspeth Grant had come up to the Highlands with a boyfriend.

The light was fading fast as Hamish walked into the garage run by Tom Morrison. There was a man in faded blue, oil-stained overalls bent over a car engine.

"Mr. Morrison?"

"I'm just about to close up. What do you want?"

He straightened up. He was a short man with a square, pleasant face and a shock of black curly hair.

"Have you heard about the murder?" asked Hamish.

"Aye, it's all over the village."

"Tell me where you were this morning."

"You mean, you think I murdered the auld scunner? No, that I did not. I was right here. My assistant, Tolly, he was here the whole time. Folks came by for petrol from the pump. I can give you their names."

"No, that'll be fine," said Hamish, not only feeling sure Tom was telling the truth but also not wanting to waste valuable time going through his list of customers. "Tell me about Mrs. Gillespie. Can you think of anyone who might have wanted to murder her?"

"My first thought," said Tom, wiping his hands on a rag, "is that it could be anyone. She was not liked. But murder! No, I can't think of a person who would do that. I've felt like it sometimes. She broke up my marriage to her stepdaughter. But it's a lang, lang way between thinking and doing."

"Will you be getting back with Heather now?" asked Hamish.

"I don't think so. She didn't trust me, and when there's no trust in a marriage, it's no good."

"If there's no jealousy in a marriage," said Hamish, "then there's no love."

"I know you, Macbeth. You're not married, so what would you know about it?"

"A lot, believe you me. Now, I want you to think hard about who she knew and who she might have been blackmailing."

"Blackmail!"

"Perhaps. There wasn't a scrap of business papers in her home. Do you happen to know if she owned any other property?"

Tom shook his head. "Better ask Heather or her father."

"I will. I'll come back tomorrow for a chat."

*   *   *

Hamish drove straight to Lochdubh. Jimmy was waiting for him outside the police station. "I thought you'd have let yourself in like everyone else does," said Hamish, unlocking the door. "You know where the spare key is kept."

"I just got here."

Hamish let him in. Then he remembered his dog and cat. Where had they gone? The last he had seen of them was when they had headed off together.

The phone in the office rang, and he went to answer it. It was Angela Brodie, the doctor's wife. "I saw your police car passing, and I've sent your animals home. They were round here mooching food. I've fed them both."

"Thanks, Angela. I've got to rush. I'll call on you tomorrow."

When Hamish returned to the kitchen, it was to find Jimmy frantically rummaging in the cupboards.

"The whisky's in the oven," said Hamish.

"What's it doing there?"

"Well, the locals come round and say, 'What about a dram?' and if I want rid of them, I say I haven't any. I've even known them to do what you were doing and start searching the cupboards, saying they're sure I have some and I've just forgotten where I put it."

Jimmy retrieved the half bottle from the oven and took down two glasses from a cupboard.

Jimmy poured a large measure for himself and a small one for Hamish. He drained his glass and filled it up again.

"That's better." He sighed. "What have you got?"

Hamish described everything he had found out.

"So," said Jimmy, "the main thing is the missing papers or letters. Safe-deposit box?"

"Oh, my, I forgot about that one."

"Don't worry. I've a feeling she wouldn't leave them there and that the manager would have told you if she had a safe-deposit box. Maybe she bought some sort of lock-up."

"Or she might just have buried them in her garden."

"There's an idea. I'll get the men onto it."

"How did you get on with Mrs. Styles?"

Jimmy poured himself more whisky. "That was quite a scene," he said. "Blair tried to bully her, and she tore into him and called him a disgrace. She said he was not a Christian. He was that furious, he was going to take her in for questioning. She phoned Daviot and said she was putting in a complaint for police harassment. Daviot pulled Blair off and suggested it would be better if the questioning was left to Hamish Macbeth. Of course, Blair agreed, hoping that Mrs. Styles would put in a complaint about you."

"I'll try her first thing in the morning." A sharp bark sounded from outside the door. Hamish opened it, and Lugs and Sonsie slouched in.

"This is interesting, the bit where that old neighbour told you that Bernie Fleming might have been murdered. How would Mrs. Gillespie know? No proof."

"She might have been cleaning at the time. Say Mrs. Fleming lost her temper and gave him an almighty push. What about the professor, now?" asked Hamish. "Silly pompous wee man that he is."

"Blair toadied to him, so we didn't get much. He was never

married. Doesn't seem to be gay. Blameless, boring life, if you ask me."

"Someone as arrogant as he is wouldn't have gone on putting up with such as Mrs. Gillespie for long."

"Could be," said Jimmy. "But by all accounts the woman was a bully. Blair's a bully and look at the way he arse-licked the old boy. Maybe she treated him well. Anyway, now that our esteemed leader thinks you have the right touch, you'll be able to have a talk with him yourself."

The kitchen door opened, and Elspeth walked in, followed by Luke Teviot. "I'm off," said Jimmy. "How're things in the big city, Elspeth?"

"Not as exciting as here. You've got a murder."

"Ask your boyfriend about it," said Jimmy, and made his escape.

"Boyfriend?" asked Luke.

"He was just joking," said Elspeth quickly.

Luke sat down at the kitchen table. "Got an ashtray in here?"

Hamish took out an ashtray from one of the cupboards and put it on the table. Luke lit a cigarette. Hamish had given up smoking a long time ago and was annoyed to find himself longing for one.

Elspeth and Hamish sat down and surveyed each other warily. Elspeth had had her frizzy hair straightened, and Hamish was not sure whether he liked it or not. She was also dressed smart-casual rather than in the usual assortment of thrift shop clothes she used to wear.

"You made it here fast," said Hamish. "You've both been sent to cover the murder?"

"No, we're here on holiday together."

"So you're an item?"

"No," said Luke, and "Yes," said Elspeth, both at the same time.

Luke noticed that Hamish now seemed amused and relaxed where a moment before he had been stiff and angry.

"The thing is," said Elspeth, "that we could both end up having a paid holiday. The news desk is keen on this."

"Why?" asked Hamish curiously. "You've got murders damn near every day in Glasgow. This is chust one auld woman who got bashed with her bucket."

"Because we happen to be up here, and a murder in the Highlands is considered more interesting, so what can you tell us?"

"Elspeth, you know the ropes. You'll both need to go to Strathbane and get the official statement. I cannae tell you anything other than the fact that, yes, she was murdered when she was leaving Professor Sander's house in Braikie. I found the body."

"Why were you there?" asked Elspeth.

"Chust happened to be passing."

"You're lying, Hamish." Elspeth's silver eyes were fixed on his face. "We've been to view the scene of the crime. The prof's house is at the end of a cul-de-sac. Bessie, the maid at the hotel, told me you'd won the services of Mrs. Gillespie in a raffle. You went to see her. What about? There's a rumour flying around that she might have been a blackmailer. Did she ferret among the police papers?"

"That's enough," said Hamish sharply. "Look, Elspeth, I'll do a deal wi' ye. Go to police headquarters. Get a statement from them. Do it by the book. But there's one thing I'll tell you: if she was a blackmailer, I can't find a letter or even bills in her house—not a bit of paper. She may have hidden them somewhere. You find out where, and I'll give you what I've got."

"You're on. Not like you not to offer us some refreshment, Hamish."

"I'm tired, and Jimmy's drunk all the whisky. Off with the pair of you."

Outside the police station, Luke said, "That policeman's keen on you. And what about you? Why did you let him think we were an item?"

"Stop asking questions. There's a good restaurant along here. I'm hungry."

Elspeth stalked off. Luke watched her, amused, and then followed after her.

Chapter Four

Everyone lives by selling something.

—Robert Louis Stevenson

Before visiting Mrs. Styles the following morning, Hamish decided to call in at the bakery in Braikie to have a talk with Mrs. Gillespie's friend Queenie Hendry. He remembered Queenie as soon as he set eyes on her. He had interviewed her once before when he was tracking down a murderer. She was a pleasant-looking middle-aged woman with neat grey hair and a rosy-cheeked face. He found it hard to believe that she should have had anything in common with the late Mrs. Gillespie.

"Can I be having a word with you?" he asked.

"It'll be about Mavis," she said. She turned to her assistant. "Alice, mind the counter."

Queenie raised the counter flap and walked through. "It's a terrible business," she said. "Poor Mavis."

"I gather you were a friend of Mrs. Gillespie."

"Yes, we often had a chat together after I'd closed up the shop. My, the poor woman did love cream cakes."

"Did you ever get the impression—now, think carefully—that she might be a blackmailer?"

She turned a little pale.

"Look," urged Hamish. "She's dead. If you know anything at all, please tell me."

"If I tell you, you'll report me to the council," she whispered.

"Come outside," said Hamish. "We need a private chat."

They walked together outside the shop. The wind had died down, and the day was warm and sunny.

"I'll do you a deal," said Hamish. "Whatever you tell me, I won't report you to the council."

She hugged herself with strong arms across her white-aproned chest.

"It's like this. I had this plague o' mice. Had a job getting rid o' the things. The shop was quiet, and I happened to tell Mavis about it. 'Let me see,' she said. 'I've a fair way with the mice.'

"I led her through to the back. I switched on the light, and there they were, mice scampering all over the place. To my horror, she took out a wee camera and started snapping off pictures. Then she said, 'Now, Queenie, I think the health and safety people at the council would be interested in these photos.' I told her the exterminator was coming in the morning, but I know there's this bastard on the council who loves making life a misery for shopkeepers. She said she wouldn't do anything about it as long as she could have a box of cream cakes every day. That wasn't enough. She insisted she was my friend and kept dropping in for a chat. She frightened me."

"You should have come to me," said Hamish. "I'd soon have shut her up. I'll need to ask you what you were doing yesterday morning."

"I was in the shop all morning. I can tell you which customers came in, and Alice was with me the whole time."

"Did it never dawn on you that if she was blackmailing you, she could have been blackmailing others?"

"No. She never asked for money. Just cream cakes."

Hamish thanked her and told her if she could think of anything else or had any idea who else Mrs. Gillespie might have been blackmailing, to let him know.

As he drove off to interview Mrs. Styles, he glanced in his rear-view mirror and noticed a small car following him with Shona Fraser at the wheel. He stopped, got out as she parked behind him, and went to speak to her.

"You should be with the detective chief inspector," he said.

"He does nothing but shout at people. I thought I'd catch up with you. I'm sure you're the better story."

Hamish leered down at her. "Aye, that would be grand. I can chust see myself on the telly. Which would you say wass my best side?"

"Forget about that. Where are you going?"

"I'm going up to the Gordons' farm to check their sheep papers are in order. Checking sheep papers is a right important thing."

"But what about the murder!"

"The sheep papers may not be important to you," said Hamish, whose face reflected nothing more than amiable stupidity, "but they're life and death to some folk. Now, let me tell you all about sheep. I haff the rare knowledge of the sheep."

"Got to go," said Shona hurriedly.

Hamish watched, amused, as she drove off. Then the smile left his face as he continued to drive towards the home of Mrs. Styles. The fact that Mrs. Gillespie could go to such lengths to blackmail Mrs. Hendry—and for cream cakes! Gluttony, malice, control, and bullying. No wonder someone murdered her!

Mrs. Styles lived in a bungalow on the outskirts of the town. He cursed Blair as he walked up to the door. Blair would have left Mrs. Styles with a dislike and distrust of the police.

Luke Teviot felt awash with tea. He found Elspeth's idea of reporting in the Highlands very odd. Instead of going to interview the people for whom Mrs. Gillespie had cleaned, she had called on various homes between Lochdubh and Braikie, being welcomed by people she had known, drinking tea, and gossiping. But he soon began to see that she was eliciting quite a bit of information about the late Mrs. Gillespie.

At last, Elspeth said, "We're going to see a Mrs. Samson. She lived next door to Mrs. Fleming and seems to have been a friend of Mrs. Gillespie as well as being a nasty gossip."

"All right," said Luke, sending a lazy spiral of cigarette smoke up into the clear air. "But if I have to drink another cup of tea or eat another scone, I'll scream."

Soon they were sitting in the smoky cavern of Mrs. Samson's living room. "Do you mind if I smoke?" asked Luke.

"Yes, I do," snapped Mrs. Samson. "Do you know what that stuff does to your lungs?"

The fire belched out another cloud of grey coal smoke.

"As I was saying," pursued Elspeth, "we are planning to write a nice obituary about your friend."

Those eyes magnified by the thick glasses seemed to grow even larger as Mrs. Samson gave a dry chuckle. Then she said, "You'll have a hard time, lassie. Nobody liked her."

"But you were her friend."

"I liked her gossip. She knew something about everyone, even you, Miss Grant. She knew you were pining after that policeman but how he never got over Miss Halburton-Smythe."

Luke raised his eyebrows in surprise. Elspeth said quickly, "Then obviously she often never got her facts straight. How did you both become friends?"

"She came to my door one day. She asked to use the phone. I said I'd seen her with one o' those mobile things, but herself said the battery was dead. I let her in. She made a call from the hall to someone. She said, 'I'm missing my wages and you'd better pay up.' That's all I heard. Now I learn from that Macbeth policeman that she was a blackmailer."

"When was this? When did she make that call?" asked Elspeth.

"Let me see. My memory isn't so good. Maybe June last year."

"So you didn't know her for long?"

"No, but she was a fair gossip. That first time, she says

to me, she says, your neighbour killed her husband. Did you know that? Well, I told her to sit down because I fair loathe that wee scunner next door with her airs and graces. Always complaining. She said the smoke from my lum had messed up her washing."

Elspeth wondered briefly how any smoke managed to get up the chimney, as most of it seemed to escape into the room.

"How did Mrs. Fleming's husband die?" asked Luke.

"Fell down the stairs and broke his neck."

"And had Mrs. Gillespie seen this?"

"She didn't say. She was always hinting at things. After she said that Mrs. Fleming had murdered her husband, she wouldn't be drawn on anything. Did she make a will?"

"I suppose so," said Elspeth. "Why?"

"Herself said she'd leave me something useful in her will."

Elspeth was now longing to get to the house next door and interview Mrs. Fleming, but she had to go on pretending she was writing an obituary.

At last, they escaped.

"Whew!" said Elspeth. "I thought I'd choke to death. I wonder if she did make a will. Let's try Mrs. Fleming. Put that cigarette out, Luke. Haven't you inhaled enough smoke already?"

Mrs. Styles was a formidable woman. She was built like a cottage loaf and had thick grey hair worn in a bun. She had a round face and large grey eyes. Her mouth was small and thin. She was wearing a tweed skirt, crepe blouse, and a long woollen cardigan.

She looked Hamish up and down and demanded, "What do you want?"

"Just a wee chat."

"I don't have time for wee chats. I have already complained about that man Blair and his manners."

"I have heard," said Hamish, "that you are an intelligent and perceptive lady. You seem to me the type of lady who might notice things other people do not."

She hesitated, and then said, "You'd better come in."

In the living room, a man was slumped in front of the television set. "Archie," said Mrs. Styles, "you'd better leave us a minute."

Her husband—Hamish assumed it was her husband—got up and shuffled out without a word. He was a small, stooped man wearing a suit, collar, and tie but with battered old carpet slippers on his feet.

"Sit down, Officer. Wait till I turn the television off. Right. Now, what do you want to know?"

Hamish sat down and looked around the living room as he did so. He found it surprising. He would have expected it to be sparkling clean, but it was messy with discarded magazines and newspapers. The fireplace was full of ash.

"I gather that Mrs. Gillespie could be a bit of a bully."

"Yes, she was, but she got nowhere with me with that sort of behaviour. I kept after her and made sure she did her job properly."

"When was she last here?"

"Five days ago."

"Did you guess she might have been blackmailing people?"

"No, I did not. Of course, she wouldn't try anything like that with me. I would have gone straight to the police."

"Were you surprised to learn she had been murdered?"

"Yes, I was. I mean, this is Braikie."

"There have been murders here in the past."

"It was probably some traveller, one of these New Age people."

"We don't get the New Age people up here," said Hamish. "The locals are liable to chase them off with shotguns."

"Well, ever since they built the new motorways, all sorts of weird people come up from the cities."

"Did Mrs. Gillespie ever talk to you about the other people she cleaned for?"

"I do not tolerate gossip. Besides, when she was here, I was usually out and about. I do a great deal for the church."

Hamish persevered but could not get any useful information out of her. As he was rising to leave, he noticed a framed photo on a side table. It was of a very beautiful young girl, standing by the wall of some seafront, her long black hair blown by the wind. "Your daughter?" he asked.

"I do not have children. Believe it or not, that was me as a young lassie."

In the small hallway just before the front door was a hat stand of the old-fashioned kind with a mirror and a ledge in front of the mirror. Hamish noticed that both the mirror and the ledge were dusty. He estimated they hadn't been cleaned for some time.

He decided to return to Lochdubh and collect his pets and then go to Strathbane and read the report on the late Mr.

Fleming's death. There seemed to be a board meeting going on inside his head. One voice was wondering whether Mrs. Styles was as innocent as she would like to appear, another querying the death of Bernie Fleming, another wondering whether Elspeth was romantically involved with Luke Teviot, and suddenly another little voice asked whether Mrs. Gillespie had left a will.

Hamish collected Lugs and Sonsie and drove quickly to Strathbane. At police headquarters, he sat down and switched on the computer and searched until he found the report of Bernie Fleming's death. He read it and reread it but it seemed an open-and-shut case. Accidental death.

He went up to the detectives' room and found Jimmy Anderson just leaving. "I've been checking up on Bernie Fleming's death," said Hamish. "Nothing there that I can see. Did Mrs. Gillespie make a will?"

"Yes, I phoned round every solicitor in Braikie until I got the right one. She left everything to her husband. Oh, and one other thing. She left a sealed packet of mementoes to be given to her friend Mrs. Samson."

"He won't have given it to her," said Hamish. "I mean, he'll have to wait for the outcome of the police enquiry."

"As a matter of fact, he gave it to her this morning. She called at his office in a cab. He said he didn't see the harm in it because it wasn't money. He's a bit young and naïve."

"We've got to get to Mrs. Samson fast!"

"Why?"

"Don't you see? Mrs. Gillespie might have left her copies

of the stuff she was using to blackmail people. We've got to get to her as quick as possible. I'll drive. You've been drinking already."

Hamish put on the siren as they raced toward Braikie. "You don't think anything could happen to her this early?" asked Jimmy, looking nervously back at Hamish's wild cat, Sonsie.

"Even if she's all right, we need to know what was in that package," said Hamish. "Oh, damn it. Sheep on the road. Get out and chase them, Jimmy."

"Chase them yourself. I'm your superior officer. I don't chase sheep."

Hamish stopped the Land Rover, and Jimmy watched, amused, as Hamish, his arms going like a windmill, sent the sheep scurrying off into a nearby field.

Hamish heaved a sigh of relief when he at last gained the shore road leading into Braikie. He screeched through the town, the siren blaring, and up to the villas where Mrs. Samson lived.

His heart sank when he turned into her street. Outside her house, it was chaos as the local fire brigade battled with the searing flames that were engulfing the house.

"Is she in there?" cried Hamish, leaping down from the Land Rover.

"Can't get near the place to find out," said a fireman. "Stand back."

Hamish made a run for the front door, but before he could reach it, the glass-paned door exploded and a great sheet of flame burst out, driving him back.

Blair arrived and demanded to know what was going on. Hamish told him that Mrs. Samson had collected a package from the solicitor that morning.

"So," explained Hamish, "someone knew about that package, and someone must have been frightened that it contained blackmailing stuff. If she made one phone call, we can trace it."

Out of the corner of his eye, Blair saw Shona arriving and said quickly, "You'd better get back round all the suspects again and find out where they were."

Hamish took one last look at the blazing house before he turned away. Old Mrs. Samson could not possibly be alive in that inferno, and whatever papers she had received from the solicitor would have gone up in flames with her.

Hamish decided to begin at the beginning and go back and see Mrs. Barret-Wilkinson. He was driving through Braikie's main street when at first he thought he saw a ghost. The elderly figure of Mrs. Samson was looking in the window of the bakery. He screeched to a halt. Lugs let out a sharp bark of protest. Hamish jumped down from the Land Rover.

"Mrs. Samson," he cried. "Do you know your house is on fire?"

"What!"

"It's in flames. I'd better take you back there. The firemen think you're still inside."

She put her hand to her chest, and he supported her, frightened she would faint. Then he helped her up into the Land

Rover. She huddled in the passenger seat, muttering, "Oh, my house."

"Was it insured?" asked Hamish.

"Aye." A little colour began to return to her cheeks. "I'll maybe be able to get myself a nice wee bungalow, everything on the one floor."

Hamish drove up to the burning villa. Elspeth saw him arrive and whipped out a camera and began to take photographs as Hamish helped the old lady out of the Land Rover.

Blair came hurrying up. "Who's this? I told you to get out there and interview folks."

"This is Mrs. Samson," said Hamish. "She was fortunately out shopping when the fire started." Hamish turned to the old lady. "Mrs. Samson, the solicitor gave you a packet of papers left you by Mrs. Gillespie. Do you by any chance have them with you?"

She shook her head. "I never even opened the packet. Mrs. Gillespie told that solicitor it was just old mementoes—photos and letters. I thought I'd give them to her stepdaughter, Heather."

"And did you?"

"I hadn't the time. I left them on the table in the hall."

Hamish looked gloomily at the blazing house.

"You!" snapped Blair. "Stop standing there gawking like a loon. Get to work. We'll look after Mrs. Samson."

Behind Blair's back, Jimmy mimed drinking motions which Hamish interpreted to mean that he would be over at Lochdubh at the end of the day.

*   *   *

Most of the time, Hamish was used to the winds of Sutherland. But as he got out of the Land Rover in front of Mrs. Barret-Wilkinson's house, he felt the increasing strength of a gale and sighed. Calm days were a brief respite from the yelling and screech of the Sutherland winds, and this one was already beginning to howl like a banshee.

He clutched at his cap as he rang the bell. He waited. No reply.

He retreated and drove down to Mrs. Beattie's shop. "Have you seen Mrs. Barret-Wilkinson this morning?" he asked.

"No, it's been right quiet. Awful that, about Mrs. Samson's house."

"How did you hear? Do you know Mrs. Samson?"

"Never heard of her, but my niece in Braikie called me a minute ago. Burnt to a crisp, the old lady was," added Mrs. Beattie with gloomy relish.

"She's fine. She was out when the fire started," said Hamish.

"There's a mercy. I see you looking at the sausage rolls. I just made them this morning."

"I'll take six," said Hamish.

Outside, he let the dog and cat out for a run and then fed them two sausage rolls each. He put them back in the Land Rover, climbed in himself, and settled down to have a lunch of sausage rolls and coffee. He had filled up a thermos flask before he left that morning. Rain smeared the windscreen. Outside, the waves were rising—sea loch waves—angrily racing in rapidly one after the other, while out in the Atlantic, the gigantic ones pounded the cliffs.

He drove back to Mrs. Barret-Wilkinson's house and waited.

He was just about to give up when she arrived in a four-wheel-drive vehicle. She looked startled to see him and then angry.

"I have nothing more to say to you," she shouted against the wind.

"I have something to say to you," said Hamish. "We'd better go indoors."

She reluctantly led the way.

"Now, what is it?" she demanded, one hand on the mantelpiece. She was wearing a fishing hat and a waxed coat—suitable clothes, and yet they looked somehow odd on her.

"Mrs. Samson's house has been burnt down."

"Who is Mrs. Samson?"

"A friend of the murdered Mrs. Gillespie. I am asking everyone she cleaned for where they were this morning."

"I consider it an impertinence. Oh, very well, I was over in Strathbane, shopping."

"Where?"

"Here and there."

"Did you buy anything? Have you any receipts?"

"No, you tiresome man. I window-shopped. I did not see anything I liked."

"Did anyone see you? Did you meet anyone you know?"

"No, no, and *no!* Now, leave me alone."

Hamish turned in the doorway. "The one good thing about it is that Mrs. Samson is alive."

The wind gave a sudden eldritch scream. Had she turned pale? It was hard to tell in the gloom of the room.

"Is she in the hospital?" she asked.

"No, she was out shopping when her house went up."

"That's good." As Hamish left, he turned once and saw her sinking down into a chair, her hat and coat still on.

Hamish decided he would need to visit that solicitor before interviewing anyone else. Someone knew very quickly that a package had been given to Mrs. Samson. He phoned Jimmy on his mobile and got the name and address of the solicitor.

He did a detour to Lochdubh and left his animals in the police station.

He negotiated the shore road into Braikie without any trouble because it was low tide.

The solicitor, James Bennet, had an office above a men's outfitters in the main street.

Hamish climbed the stone stairs, opened a frosted-panelled glass door, and went inside. A small girl was typing busily at a computer.

"You're to go right in," she said without looking up.

Hamish walked into the inner office. James Bennet looked up in surprise. "I'm expecting a Mrs. Withers. Didn't Eileen tell you?"

"If you mean the wee lassie outside, she didn't even look up," said Hamish. "But I've a few questions to ask you. If Mrs. Gillespie left a package in her will for Mrs. Samson, why did you let her have it before this murder case is solved?"

Mr. Bennet was a fairly young man with what Hamish's mother would call "a nice wide-open face." He was wearing a well-tailored Harris tweed suit. His black hair was neatly barbered, and he was wearing spectacles. Hamish wondered if the lenses were plain glass to give the young man an air of authority, because he could spot no magnification.

James Bennet sighed. "I did not give away anything mentioned in the will. I already told the police this. The morning she was found murdered, Mrs. Gillespie called and said she wanted me to give the package to Mrs. Samson. I told her to give it to the woman herself, but she said time was running out and she was rushed. I phoned Mrs. Samson and asked her whether I should put it in the post, but she said she would come round and collect it. She arrived the morning of the fire in a taxi, which she kept waiting, picked up the package, and went off again."

Hamish sat down slowly in the visitor's chair. "It seems to me," he said, "as if Mrs. Gillespie thought her life might be in danger."

"Och, she was a weird woman, always hinting at things, the sort of 'if you knew what I know' sort of thing without ever saying anything specific."

Hamish suddenly struck his forehead. The young solicitor looked at him in surprise.

"There wasnae a scrap of paper in her house," said Hamish, his accent thickening as it always did when he was angry or excited. "I mean, bankbooks, house deeds, bills, things like that. Do you have them?"

James looked around his cluttered office. "Oh, yes, they're all here somewhere."

I'm losing my touch, thought Hamish. But he said angrily, "Why didn't you inform the police?"

"They didn't ask me."

"I'll need to take them with me."

"Have you a warrant?"

"Don't be daft, laddie, and waste my time. Hand them over."

"I'll need a receipt."

"Of course, you'll get a receipt."

"Eileen!" called James.

His secretary came in. Her hair was gelled into spikes, and she wore a low-cut blouse exposing an area of freckled bosom. Although she was young, her face was already set in a sullen look. Her make-up was as thick as a papier-mâché carnival mask.

"Get the box with Mrs. Gillespie's papers."

"Okey-dokey."

Hamish waited anxiously. The wind rattled the window-panes, and a smouldering coal fire in an old Victorian fireplace suddenly burst into flame.

At last, Eileen returned with a large deed box.

"I think you'll find everything is in there," said James.

"Did she have an accountant?" asked Hamish.

"Not as far as I know. She wouldn't need one. She probably never paid taxes. She must have earned very little cleaning houses."

"She had a tidy sum of money. Didn't you look?"

"No, why should I? As far as I was concerned, she was eccentric, and if she wanted to go on paying me to keep all her papers, I was quite happy."

Hamish wrote out a receipt, thanked him, and left, clutching the box. He decided to look at the contents first before turning them over to police headquarters.

Elspeth and Luke had begged the use of a desk in the *Highland Times*, the local newspaper with an office in Lochdubh, and were busy filing a joint story.

"Are you sweet on that copper?" asked Luke when they finished.

"Of course not," said Elspeth. "I knew him when I used to work up here."

Luke studied the smoke rising up from his cigarette and drifting over the No Smoking sign on the wall. "I thought you were. There was a sort of atmosphere."

"Get this straight," said Elspeth angrily. "Hamish Macbeth was once engaged to Priscilla Halburton-Smythe. Her parents own the hotel we're staying at. He never got over her."

"Dumped him, did she?"

"No, strange to say, *he* dumped *her*."

"So why . . . ?"

"Leave it, Luke."

In the police station office, Hamish opened the box and began to go through the contents. He found the deeds to the house, electricity and gas bills up to the previous month, and a bankbook showing the amount of money he already knew about from the printout. But no blackmailing material.

He phoned Jimmy and told him of the find and said he would deliver the box to police headquarters. "Don't bother," said Jimmy. "I'll come over and collect it. If I don't get some time away from Blair, I'll strangle him."

Hamish went along to the general store and bought a bottle of whisky. Angela Brodie, the doctor's wife, was buying cat food.

Her thin face lit up when she saw Hamish. "How are things going, Hamish? We hardly see you these days—that is, unless you want to offload your animals onto me."

"Sorry. I'll be round soon. How's the writing going?"

"Slowly and painfully." Angela had won a literary award for her first novel. "Getting that award didn't give me confidence. It did the opposite. I feel I can't match up to the first book. If this murder case you're on ever gets solved, would you read some of it for me? Tell me what you think?"

"I'm no literary critic."

"But you're a reader."

"All right."

"What's the whisky for?"

"Jimmy Anderson," said Hamish. "I'd better feed him as well."

"I wouldn't bother," said Angela, who knew Jimmy of old. "Whisky is food as well as drink to that man."

Hamish returned to the police station, where he cooked up some venison liver for the dog and cat before making himself a sandwich and a cup of tea. He had just finished eating when Jimmy arrived, cursing the solicitor for not having told them about the papers he was holding.

"And he gave me the impression that the package was left

for Mrs. Samson in the will. Anything blackmailable in there?" he asked.

"Nothing. Sit down and I'll get you a dram. The bankbook's interesting. The cash payments started two years ago—at first just a few modest payments in her checquing account, then they begin to increase. Maybe she hinted at something and one of them cracked and paid her money and she realised she was on to a good little earner. I think she was blackmailing more than one person. I think she was blackmailing several. We'll need to dig into the backgrounds of everyone she cleaned for." Hamish poured a measure of whisky into a glass and put it on the kitchen table next to Jimmy.

A particularly thunderous roar of wind shook the police station. "I don't know how you can bear that wind," grumbled Jimmy. "We're protected by the surrounding buildings in Strathbane, but up here, the noise wears a man down."

"The gales are getting worse," said Hamish. "And the waves are getting higher. I hope I don't live to see Lochdubh washed away."

"Dead-alive hole," said Jimmy callously. "Wouldn't be any great loss. Now, let's start with Professor Sander."

"What did you make of him?" asked Hamish.

"Prissy little man. Furious with us for asking questions."

"What's he a professor of?"

"Was. Retired. English was his subject. He produced a popular biog called *Byron: The Tortured Years*. Did well. Hasn't done anything since. Never married."

"Might be an idea to check the Sex Offenders Register."

"We screwed up in Scotland, remember? About six thousand sex offenders before 1997 weren't put on the list. Still, it's worth a look."

"Which university was he at?"

"Strathbane."

"Hardly an academic place. I believe they even give degrees in car maintenance these days."

"Blair's got a team of coppers out ferreting around. No one saw anyone near Mrs. Samson's house before it went up in flames. But the fire chief thinks the fire started at the back door, and anyone could get to that over the fields."

"Arson?"

"Not sure yet. Takes ages."

"Where's Mrs. Samson going to stay?"

"They're putting her up at the old folks' home, High Haven, for the moment. She can't buy anything else until she gets the insurance money."

"I forgot to ask the solicitor how large the package was," said Hamish. "She was carrying a large handbag. If she's still got the stuff and if it contains blackmail material, her life could be in danger."

"Why worry?" asked Jimmy. "One blackmailer less would please me."

"Aye, but it would be another murder to solve. Did you interview any of the folk she cleaned for?"

"Apart from the professor, I went with Blair to interview Mrs. Fleming. Blair was all over her. He told me afterwards she was like a fairy."

"She's a fairy who threw a vase at me," said Hamish. "She

lives quite near. She could have nipped over the garden fence and poured petrol through the back door."

"Then there's Mrs. Styles, the one that Blair fell foul of. What about your Mrs. Wellington?"

"Mrs. Gillespie found out that the minister delivered an old sermon one Sunday and hinted that it would be awful if folks found out. Got nowhere with that. Mrs. Barret-Wilkinson, now. She interests me. I've a feeling she's playing the country lady. But she's the one that lives furthest away."

"We've run a police check already on all of them," said Jimmy, reaching for the whisky bottle. "Nothing there."

"I wonder if any of them got into the local newspaper over anything," said Hamish. "Maybe I'll walk along and have a look. No, you are not getting any more whisky, Jimmy, and take that box of stuff over to police headquarters."

"Here's lover boy," said Luke.

Elspeth looked up and flushed slightly as Hamish walked into the newspaper office.

"I need your help," said Hamish.

"And we need yours." Luke was sitting next to Elspeth, and he draped a long arm around her shoulders. "We just filed a story, but it's very thin."

"You'll get what I've got when I get it," said Hamish. "Elspeth knows that. All right. It'll soon come out, so you can have this, only don't quote me. Mrs. Samson collected a packet from the solicitor. Mrs. Gillespie had left it with him, saying she wanted it posted to Mrs. Samson. The solicitor phoned Mrs. Samson, who took a cab round on the day of the fire and picked up the package herself. Now, if Mrs. Gillespie was a blackmailer—and that's sheer speculation, although she had more in her bank account than a cleaner should have—someone might have thought Mrs. Samson now had incriminating papers and set her house on fire. The solicitor is a Mr. James Bennet. I'll give you his phone number. Phone him for confirmation, and then about the blackmail business put it down to 'sources' in Braikie. Oh, and ask the solicitor what size the package was. Mrs. Samson says she never even looked at it and it was in the house when it burned down, but she could be lying and it could be in the large handbag she was carrying."

"Great stuff," said Luke. "I'll get onto it, Elspeth, if you help the copper here with what he wants."

"What is it you want, Hamish?" asked Elspeth, shrugging Luke's arm off her shoulders.

"I want to check the newspaper files to see if any of the suspects ever did anything worth a mention."

"You don't need me," said Elspeth. "You need Terry the Geek. Terry!"

A thin young man with a bad case of acne and hair as red as Hamish's came to join them from the back of the office.

"This is Terry," said Elspeth. "Mrs. MacKay's boy. He's organised the whole system."

"I didn't recognise you," said Hamish. "It seems the last time I saw you, you were just a lad."

Terry grinned sheepishly. "How can I help you?"

"I've some names I want you to look up," said Hamish. "I want to see if any of them appeared in the newspaper at any time."

"Come over to my computer, and I'll search for you."

"I can't see how it can work," said Hamish. "I mean, won't it be a long job of trawling through paper after paper?"

"Not a bit of it," said Terry proudly. "I've organised it by names, places, and subject."

"Let's start." Hamish sat down beside him in front of a computer. "Mrs. Fiona Fleming, formerly Mrs. Bernie Fleming."

Terry's long bony fingers flicked over the keys. "Do you mind being called Terry the Geek?" asked Hamish. "Highland nicknames can be a bit cruel."

"I take it as a compliment. Anyway, this lot in Lochdubh couldn't tell one end of a computer from another."

"Some of them got computers when they were all trying to write books."

"Aye, but the novelty soon wore off and highland lethargy settled in. Here we are. Her husband fell downstairs. Verdict: accidental death."

"I know that one. Anything else?"

"Seems to be all."

"What have you got on Mrs. Mavis Gillespie?"

"Wait a bit. Oh, here's something. Last year she was down in Strathbane shopping. Speeding car mounted the pavement and nearly killed her. She jumped back just in time."

"Let me see."

Terry angled the screen towards Hamish. Hamish looked at the date. The incident had taken place in August the previous year when he was off on a fishing holiday.

Mrs. Gillespie had been waiting to cross the road at the junction of Glebe Street and Thomson Street. She had leapt back just in time. She said she was so shocked that the make of the car hadn't registered with her. She said it was large and black. Police decided the driver had probably been drunk, for who would want to kill Mrs. Gillespie?

"I'll get the police reports on that," muttered Hamish.

"Here's something else," exclaimed Terry. "She was at the clay pigeon shoot down at Moy Hall, outside Inverness. That was January this year. She said a bullet whizzed past her, missing her by centimetres."

Hamish studied the report. The police did not seem to have taken any action whatsoever.

"That seems to be all," said Terry.

So that might explain why she turned the papers or whatever she had over to Mrs. Samson, thought Hamish.

She thought her life was in danger! She wanted to leave some proof of the reason for it behind.

Chapter Five

I waive the quantum o' the sin,
The hazard of concealing;
But och; it hardens a' within,
And petrifies the feeling!

—Robert Burns

Hamish suddenly realised that he had not seen Matthew Campbell, the local reporter who was married to Lochdubh's schoolteacher. "Where's Matthew?" he called over to Elspeth.

"On vacation," she called back. "He'll be furious at missing all this."

"But we're not, are we, darling?" said Luke, and kissed her on the cheek.

Hamish turned back to Terry, his accent suddenly more marked. "Chust let us get on with this. Whit about Professor Sander?"

But apart from a short paragraph two years ago saying that the professor had given a lecture on Byron at the Braikie high school, there was nothing else. Mrs. Styles was mentioned various times in connection with church works, and there was nothing at all on Mrs. Barret-Wilkinson.

Hamish thanked Terry. He stopped beside Elspeth. "A wee word wi' you in private."

"Okay, we've just finished."

They walked together outside. "Is that your fellow?" shouted Hamish, but the screaming gale whipped his words away.

By unspoken consent, they hurried along to the local bar. "What?" demanded Elspeth when they were inside. "No, I haven't time for a drink. What is it?"

"Is that your fellow?"

"What's it got to do with you?"

Hamish suddenly felt silly. "Chust wondered."

"Then go on wondering," said Elspeth, and shot out of the door.

Hamish saw Archie Maclean, the fisherman, sitting at a table beside the peat fire.

He bought himself a tonic water and went to join him.

"Wimmin trouble?" asked Archie.

"No, it iss chust this case I'm working on."

"You know," said Archie, "I haff been thinking. It iss all around the village that the auld woman, Gillespie, might ha' been a blackmailer, but I haff the ither idea."

"That being?" The high colour caused by Elspeth's last remark was slowly subsiding in Hamish's face.

"It iss this. It wass not the blackmailing at all, at all. It wass the cleaning."

"Cleaning?"

"Aye. Now, look at my missus. She cleans and cleans and scrubs and polishes from sunup to sundown and, man, I tell you, Hamish Macbeth, there haff been the times when I haff had the evil thoughts."

Hamish looked sympathetically at Archie in his tight suit. The locals said his wife even boiled his suits in the wash, and Archie always carried around with him an aroma of old-fashioned carbolic soap and disinfectant.

"Archie, there are times when we all feel like murdering someone, but we don't do it."

"Aye, but there is nothing like soap and water and scrubbing for tipping a man over the edge."

Hamish suddenly decided to go back and see Mr. Gillespie. But when he arrived at the housing estate, he could see police tape across the front of the garden. Jimmy was standing outside, smoking.

"What's going on?" asked Hamish.

"We're digging up the garden in case she might have buried a box of stuff there."

"I'm beginning to think Mrs. Gillespie knew her life was in danger and the packet given to Mrs. Samson contained the genuine articles." Hamish told Jimmy about what might have been two attempts on Mrs. Gillespie's life. "All the bankbooks and stuff were in that box I gave you."

Hamish then went to Heather Gillespie's bungalow, but she wasn't at home. He decided to go to the hospital and talk to Dr. Renfrew. Perhaps Mrs. Gillespie had been blackmailing him over his alleged affair with Mrs. Fleming.

He had to wait an hour before Dr. Renfrew appeared. Hamish looked at him in surprise. He had expected someone handsome. But Dr. Renfrew was small and tubby with thinning hair, gold-rimmed spectacles, podgy hands, and an arrogant manner.

"I hope you have a very good reason for disturbing me, Officer," he said.

"Are you having an affair with Mrs. Fiona Fleming?" asked Hamish bluntly.

"This is outrageous. You come in here and—"

Hamish interrupted. "Just answer the question."

"Of course not. I have a good mind to sue you for slander."

"Then you'd better sue most of Braikie as well," said Hamish. "The reason I am asking is because the late Mrs. Gillespie appears to have been a blackmailer. Did she come after you?"

"I have nothing to hide. I lead a blameless life. Good day, Officer!"

Hamish drove out of Braikie and up into the hills. He parked the Land Rover and let the dog and cat out into the heather for a run. He found a flat rock jutting out of the heather and sat down on it and stared out over Braikie. So many suspects. His thoughts were being hampered by a reluctant appreciation of the murderer. Mrs. Gillespie had been a vile woman. Still, murder was murder. He wondered whether Mrs. Samson was still at risk. He phoned Jimmy and asked if anyone was checking on her.

"There's a police guard on her," said Jimmy. "What are you doing now?"

"I think I'll go to Strathbane University and see if I can dig up anything on the professor's past. See if there's anyone there old enough to remember him. Don't tell Blair."

Strathbane University was a dismal Stalinist sort of building, put up in the fifties when most architects seem to have been in love with concrete. White-faced, unhealthy-looking students roamed its corridors. Hamish found his way to the bursar's office. The bursar, Mrs. Pilkington, was an efficient-looking grey-haired woman. "I'll check the records," she said in answer to Hamish's request. She switched on a computer on her desk.

At last, she said, "Professor Sander came here from Glasgow University in 1992. He retired from here five years ago."

"Why did he leave a big university like Glasgow to come here?"

"That I do not know."

"Is there anyone who might remember him? Someone he might have been friendly with?"

"I'm new to the job here. You could ask my predecessor, Mrs. Black. I'll give you her address."

Mrs. Black lived in a croft house outside Strathbane on the Ullapool road.

When Hamish explained the reason for his visit, she invited him in. Like most croft houses, hers was very small, with a stone-flagged living room. Mrs. Black was an energetic, white-haired woman with a shrewd, intelligent face.

"I'll make us some tea," she said. "Sit down by the fire."

Hamish looked around as she hurried off to the kitchen counter at the opposite side of the room. There was one good landscape painting over the fireplace and bookshelves crammed into every available space.

"Do you have sheep?" he asked.

"Yes, I do have sheep, and I'm going to sell the lot at the next sheep sales in Lairg. I'd only played at it before, helping out crofter friends. It's more bother than it's all worth."

She brought over two mugs of tea and set them on a coffee table in front of the fire and then sat down opposite Hamish.

"So what do you want to know about Professor Sander?"

"Could anyone have been blackmailing him?"

"I shouldn't think so. Fussy little man. Always complaining about something or another. How things were better at Glasgow University and so on until one day I shouted at him, 'Why don't you go back there?' He didn't bother me much after that."

"Not attracted to any of the students?"

"Nothing like that. I don't think he liked them. Oh, wait a bit. There was something. I'd nearly forgotten. A chap turned up one day, and I could hear him shouting that Sander had stolen his work. That book on Byron. But he was shabby and dirty, and I think he was a junkie with delusions. Nobody paid any heed to his allegations, and we never saw him again."

"If Sander *had* stolen someone's work, that would be a

motive for blackmail," said Hamish. "I mean, that was really the only work he produced."

"It'll be hard to prove unless you find the young man. I know, he came to me first and I took a note of his name before directing him to Sander's office."

"Where did you take a note?"

"Just on a pad on my desk."

"You wouldn't happen to have kept the notebook?"

"If I did, it's up in the loft with all the other papers. When I cleared my desk, I just threw everything into two large boxes."

"May I look?"

"You'll need to go up there yourself. My legs aren't what they used to be."

She led Hamish into the small hall and pulled down a folding ladder. Hamish climbed up and raised the trapdoor. He heaved himself into the loft and crawled towards two boxes standing among a jumble of discarded furniture and odds and ends. He propelled them to the loft opening, stood on the ladder, and lifted out one carton, carried it down, and then went back for the other.

"You'd better let me look," said Mrs. Black. "I might recognise that notebook unless I threw it away. Lift the boxes through to the table at the window. I don't want to have to be bending over the things."

Hamish did as he was told and waited impatiently while she slowly took out one item after the other. His stomach gave a rumble. He longed for a really filling, stodgy meal.

At last, she said, "I think this is it." She lifted out a yellow notepad. She took it over to her seat by the fire and began to go through it. "Yes, this is it," she said. "Sean Abercrombie to see Professor Sander, March 10, 1996. Yes, I remember now. This Sean looked pretty awful, but he was politely spoken and said he had been a student of the professor's at Glasgow University. I even took a note of his address. Here it is. I'll tear this page out for you."

Hamish looked at the address. Forty-five John Street, Inverness.

"Thanks," he said. "I'll just put these boxes back for you."

"Leave them. Now they're down here, I'd like a chance to go through them. Call back and let me know how you get on." Mrs. Black ushered him out.

Hamish decided that food came first. He remembered seeing a fish-and-chip shop on the outskirts of Strathbane. He drove there and studied the menu. He decided to forgo such Scottish delicacies as Mars bar and chips, Bounty bar and chips, deep-fried pizza slice and chips, and all the other things that made Scotland the unhealthiest place in the world, and settled for a haggis and chips for himself, white pudding and chips for Lugs, and fish and chips for Sonsie.

By the time they had all eaten, it was getting dark, but he decided he could not bear to wait until the following day before finding Sean Abercrombie and took the long road down to Inverness.

John Street was down by the Caledonian Canal. Number 45 was one of the neat little houses with gardens that had replaced the tower blocks.

He rang the bell. The door was answered by a middle-aged

man with a shock of white hair. He was dressed in a checked shirt, stained grey trousers, and carpet slippers.

"Paid the parking ticket," he shouted. "Police harassment, that's what this is!"

"Nothing like that," said Hamish soothingly. "Does Sean Abercrombie live here?"

"Not any longer. My boy is dead."

"May I come in?"

"No."

"Look, what happened to your son?"

"Drug overdose, the silly wee mucker. I slaved to give that boy all the opportunities I never had. He was brilliant at school. Got a scholarship to Glasgow University. Then he got on the drugs."

"Your son seemed to think that a certain Professor Sander had stolen his work."

"He was always raving on about something. Before the end, he'd go out at night calling to the aliens and shouting at the sky, 'Come and take me home. The experiment is over.' Fair broke my heart."

"Did he leave any papers, any manuscripts?"

"That he did. I made a big pile o' them and burnt the lot."

"Have you a photograph of him I could borrow? I'll give you a receipt for it. One of the latest ones would be best."

"What's this about?"

"Maybe Sean was telling the truth and this professor did steal his work."

"You'll find out it was nothing but havers. Oh, wait there. I'll get you a photograph."

After a short time, he returned with a photograph. Hamish studied it in the light shining out from the doorway. It was a photo of Sean in front of the house. He had a head of black hair gelled so that it stuck up all over the place. He had studs in his ears and a stud in his nose. He was dressed entirely in black. His face seemed set in a perpetual sneer.

"Thanks," said Hamish, touching his cap.

Now, he thought as he drove back to Lochdubh, I'll take this photo to Professor Sander tomorrow and study his reaction.

Elspeth was waiting for him when he arrived at the police station. As he opened the car door, she wrinkled her nose.

"Have you been buying up a whole fish-and-chip shop?"

"What do you want?" asked Hamish, going round and opening the back to let the dog and cat out. He was still angry with her for the way she had stormed out of the pub.

"Just a chat."

"Where's your boyfriend?"

Elspeth opened her mouth to say Luke wasn't her boyfriend, but decided against it. Let Hamish Macbeth think there were other men interested in her.

"Resting," she said.

Hamish filled the animals' water bowls. "I can't tell you anything, Elspeth. Not yet. You know what Blair is like. He's always looking for some excuse to get me into trouble."

"Maybe I've got some bits and pieces that might help you. Or not. Mrs. Styles, like Mrs. Wellington, seems absolutely blameless. I can't find out anything about Mrs. Barret-Wilkinson. Luke and I went to see her. The only mystery

I can think of is why a divorced woman—she said she was divorced . . ."

"Missed that," said Hamish, lighting the stove. "Sometimes I forget to ask the obvious. Go on."

"Why a single woman should want to shut herself away in such a remote place. She goes away occasionally—to London, the locals think—but she does not seem to have any friends in the north. But she seems a pretty strong character, and I can't see Mrs. Gillespie threatening her in any way.

"Now, Professor Sander. He huffed and puffed and told us to get lost. I sense something sleazy about that man.

"Mrs. Fleming seems the obvious one. According to the local gossips, she's having an affair with Dr. Renfrew. He's rich. Maybe she's planning to be the next Mrs. Renfrew. Maybe she pushed her husband down the stairs, and Mrs. Gillespie guessed or found out something. You see, to all her clients, she was just a cleaning woman. Then after she's ingratiated herself, she starts opening drawers and reading letters. She can't have tried to blackmail Mrs. Fleming over the affair with Dr. Renfrew because that seems to be general knowledge."

"Maybe Mrs. Fleming didn't know that." Hamish threw some slabs of peat onto the blazing kindling in the stove and put the iron lid down.

He turned and looked at Elspeth. Her hair was beginning to frizz up in the old way, and her Gypsy eyes gleamed silver. He felt that treacherous tug of attraction.

"Why don't I change and take you out for dinner?" he said suddenly.

"Can't," said Elspeth. "Luke's waiting for me. And have you forgotten the time? It's eleven o'clock."

"Then you'd better run along."

Hamish decided the following morning to visit Mrs. Samson before tackling the professor. He would need to impress on her that if that package had not gone up in the flames, then her life was at risk.

High Haven had once been a hotel, and five years ago it became an old folks' home. Hamish always found such places depressing. For one thing, the walls were usually painted in pink and blue pastel colours as if for a children's kindergarten.

He asked at the reception desk for Mrs. Samson and was told she was resting in her room. A nurse was summoned to show him the way.

The first thing Hamish noticed as they walked into the corridor where Mrs. Samson's room was located was that there was no policeman on duty.

"Where's the policeman?" he asked.

"He got called back to police headquarters yesterday evening," said the nurse. "That's Mrs. Samson's room." She knocked on the door. "Visitor for you!"

There was no reply. "Must be asleep," said the nurse, opening the door. Then she let out a gasp and put her hand to her mouth.

The small room had been ransacked. Even the mattress had been ripped open.

And lying in the middle of the mess was the dead body of Mrs. Samson.

Hamish checked for a pulse but found none. He backed out of the room and called Jimmy.

While he waited for the whole murder circus to arrive, he wondered which one of the suspects could have been terrified enough to murder Mrs. Samson. Surely not Mrs. Fleming. The verdict on her husband's death had been accident and would stay that way. He doubted if any evidence that she had murdered him would come to light. And the affair with Dr. Renfrew? Surely she must know by now that her affair was pretty general knowledge. Which one of them had such a momentous secret? The professor? Sheer vanity might have driven him to it. It seemed the only thing in his life of any merit was that book on Byron.

He could hear sirens approaching. He waited until Blair, followed by the director of the home, Mr. Beesley, came hurrying along the corridor.

Hamish explained briefly what he had found and how he suspected the duty policeman had been lured away. Cursing horribly, Blair stood aside to let the pathologist do her work.

Hamish walked to the reception desk and asked the nurse on duty if she could check her records and see if anyone had visited Mrs. Samson in the last twenty-four hours.

She shook her head after checking her computer.

He walked outside and met Jimmy. "Now what?" said Jimmy. "We'll really have the press on our backs now. You had a look at her? How did she die? Strangled? Clubbed? Poisoned?"

"I don't know," said Hamish. "Her face looked peaceful. The room had been taken to bits. I've a feeling that whoever was looking for that package didn't find it. I'm sure that's the reason her room was ransacked. Maybe she wasn't murdered. Maybe she was just threatened and got a heart attack."

Shona Fraser arrived. Jimmy was amused to see that Hamish's features became almost moronic as she approached.

"What's going on?" she asked.

"You will need to be asking Mr. Blair," said Hamish. "A verra clever man. He'll fill you in on all the details. Jimmy?"

Hamish walked a little away and then whispered, "I'd better get around the suspects again and find out where they were. I'll start with the professor."

"You do that," said Jimmy. "I'll wait here and then get some men to go around the rest of them."

Professor Sander answered the door of his home and scowled at Hamish. "I have told the police over and over again about my movements. If this continues, I will need to put in a complaint to the Police Commission."

"There's been a new development," said Hamish. "Mrs. Samson, who was a friend of Mrs. Gillespie's, has been found dead and her room ransacked. So you see, sir, we have to go around everyone again and ask them where they were during the last twenty-four hours."

"I was here," said the professor petulantly, "working on my book. Wait a minute, not all the time. I went to Inverness last evening to see an old friend, Mr. Beresford. We had dinner and I came back late, about midnight."

Hamish took out his notebook. "I will need Mr. Beresford's phone number and address."

"Wait there."

So Hamish waited, feeling the first nip of cold in the air. The long Scottish winter would soon arrive. A flock of rooks swirled up to the sky above, cawing harshly. Somewhere down the road a dog barked shrilly and then was silent.

The professor returned and handed him a slip of paper. "There! Now, if that is all . . . ?"

"Not quite. Where were you this morning?"

"Here!"

Hamish fished out the photograph of Sean Abercrombie. "Do you recognise this young man?"

The professor glanced at it. "No."

"You should. Some time ago when you were at Strathbane University, he paid you a visit and accused you of having plagiarised his work."

Professor Sander's face turned red. "Oh, that young idiot. Mad as a hatter. I had to get the university security to get rid of him."

"And was that the last you heard from him? Did he try to contact you afterwards, write to you?"

"No. And if you produce him, you will see that his brain is fried with drugs."

"He's dead."

Hamish could have sworn he saw a flicker of relief in the professor's eyes.

"That's all for now," said Hamish.

"That's all forever as far as you're concerned," said the professor, and slammed the door.

＊　　＊　　＊

Hamish realised he was tired and hungry. Police and detectives would be going round all the suspects. He phoned Jimmy. "Any news of how she died?"

"Dr. Forsythe says it looks like a heart attack. Blair's putting that out to the press and not saying anything about the ransacked room. Should keep things a bit quiet for now."

Not for long, thought Hamish. He was sure Elspeth would be already trying to pick up gossip from relatives and friends of the staff.

"Jimmy, I think the professor is a good suspect. I found out a student was claiming that Sander stole his book. The boy's dead now, drug overdose. I told the professor that, and I could swear he was relieved. Now, if the boy, Sean Abercrombie, had written to the professor with his accusations and Mrs. Gillespie found that letter, he might have paid her to keep quiet. Are you checking the bank accounts of the suspects for cash withdrawals?"

"Working on it."

"Let me know. I need some time off to think. Tell Blair I'm following leads."

Chapter Six

Marriage is a step, so grave and decisive that it attracts light-headed, variable men by its very awfulness.

—Robert Louis Stevenson

Hamish returned to Lochdubh and went straight to the newspaper office in search of Terry the Geek.

Terry was sitting with his feet on his desk, drinking apple juice and eating a whole-wheat salad sandwich.

He grinned when he saw Hamish. "Looking for Elspeth?"

"No, I need your help. It's not very legal. But I'd rather you came with me to the police station and did it there."

"Sounds like fun." Terry finished his sandwich and followed Hamish along to the police station. In the office, Hamish switched on the computer. "Here's what I want you to do, Terry. First of all, I would like you to try to access the forensic report and autopsy report on Mrs. Gillespie's death."

"Can't you just ask for them?"

"It would take too much time, and even if I finally got

them, Blair would be shouting at me to keep to my part of the job."

"All right. Anything else?"

"There was, I believe, probably a request put into the procurator fiscal for permission to view the suspects' bank accounts. See if there's anything on results."

"Leave me to it."

Hamish did not feel like asking Jimmy for any more information because Jimmy would demand whisky and Hamish felt guilty about the idea of the detective driving back to Strathbane when he was over the limit.

He decided to visit Angela Brodie. He let the dog and cat out for a run, telling them not to follow him. He felt Angela had had enough of their company.

The doctor's wife was, as usual, sitting at the end of a cluttered kitchen table, scowling at her computer.

"Can't you get a desk somewhere?" exclaimed Hamish. "How can you concentrate among the cats and the dirty dishes?"

"Sit down, Hamish. I can work better in the kitchen than anywhere else. Coffee?"

"No, thank you," said Hamish. He wasn't over-fussy about germs, but the sight of Angela's cats lying on the table amongst the breakfast debris put him off.

"Am I interrupting you?" asked Hamish.

Angela switched off the computer with a sigh. "No, I'm glad of a break. How's the case going?"

"Too many suspects and not enough clues."

"Have you seen Mrs. Gillespie's bank statements?"

"Yes."

"So was she a blackmailer?"

"She certainly had more money than she could have possibly earned. It came in a few hundred from time to time. No large amount."

"I've heard she was a ferocious bingo player," said Angela. "Are you sure she wasn't just lucky?"

Hamish stared at her, his mouth open. Then he said, "Where did she play bingo?"

"At the Catholic church hall in Braikie on Thursday nights."

Hamish groaned. "I'd better get over there. Who runs it?"

"Ask the priest, Father McNulty."

"I'm off. Damn! If it turns out the woman was chust lucky at the bingo, that blows the whole motive and a raft o' suspects clear out o' the water."

Hamish went back to the police station. Terry was still working busily. "It'll take a wee bit of time," he called.

"Stick with it," said Hamish. "I've got to go to Braikie."

He whistled for his dog and cat and put them in the Land Rover and set off for Braikie.

The Catholic church, St. Mary's, was situated up a side street off the main street. It was a modest, unassuming building, flanked on one side by the church hall and by the priest's home on the other.

He went up to the priest's house and knocked on the door. Father McNulty himself answered. He was a small, bespectacled man with a perpetually worried look.

"It's about the bingo," said Hamish.

"Oh, not again," groaned the priest. "The Free Presbyterians are aye whining about gambling."

"No, it's something else."

"Come in. I was just about to have a cup of tea."

Hamish followed him into a gloomy living-room-cum study. A large desk was heaped with papers, and the walls were lined with bookshelves. A card table was set up in front of the fire with a squat teapot and one cup and saucer.

"I'll get another cup," said Father McNulty.

Hamish waited impatiently until he returned. "Pull a chair over to the table," said the priest, "and help yourself. Now, what do you want to know about the bingo?"

"Did the late Mrs. Gillespie win much at bingo?"

"The poor woman that was murdered? Yes, she did from time to time. She was lucky."

"How much are the prizes?"

"We have a good attendance. Not big prizes, but often three or four hundred pounds."

"Was she a member of your congregation?"

"No, not many of them who come to the bingo are."

Hamish sipped his tea and winced. It was very strong. "The thing is," he said, "she had more in the bank account than she should have. I assumed she had been blackmailing people. So if the money came from lucky wins on bingo, that puts paid to that idea. Did you pay cash?"

"Yes. But if that were the case, why was her friend Mrs. Samson killed?"

"We don't know yet if she was killed. It looked like a heart attack. But you're right! Her room was ransacked, and she had retrieved a package of something from Mrs. Gillespie on the morning after Mrs. Gillespie was murdered. Someone obviously wanted what was in that package very badly."

The priest had a mild, gentle look. "Perhaps what she wanted was power."

"Explain."

"Perhaps money wasn't the main motive. Mrs. Gillespie had been a cleaner for a long time. Then she starts to snoop around. Imagine what it would mean to her to suddenly have her employers—her rich employers—dancing to her tune. Maybe a bit of money here and there, yes, but irritating other things. Maybe she wants a run down to Inverness, and one of them has to drop everything and take her. Maybe she sees an ornament and knows it's a prized possession and demands it. Things like that. Mrs. Gillespie, you see, was not liked."

Hamish suddenly remembered Queenie Hendry. All Mrs. Gillespie had demanded was cream cakes. He realised it should have struck him as surprising at the time that she had not demanded more.

"Do you know anyone she worked for who might have moved out of the area?"

"There was a Mrs. Forest. She left to live in Cnothan."

Hamish had a sudden idea. "Who runs the bingo? You?"

"No, one of my parishioners, Miss Creedy."

"I would like a word with her."

"She works in the gift shop in the main street. Why do you want to see her?"

"Is there any way the bingo could be rigged?"

"My dear man! Miss Creedy is a decent woman."

"It's amazing what decent women will do if they're being blackmailed."

The gift shop was called the Treasure Box. The window held a display of tartan dishcloths, tartan tea cosies, paperweights, and a jumble of other touristy items. Hamish wondered how the shop survived. Braikie had few tourists. The postcards in the rack beside the door were bleached by the weather.

Hamish opened the door and went in. There were no customers. "Miss Creedy?" he asked the woman behind the counter.

"Yes. What is it, Officer?"

Miss Creedy was very thin. She was wearing two sweaters and a tweed skirt. The shop was cold. She had a long, indeterminate sort of face and anxious brown eyes. Her hair was dyed an improbable shade of gold.

Hamish plunged right in. "The late Mrs. Gillespie was very lucky at the bingo."

"Yes, very lucky."

"Did it not strike you as unusual that someone should win so often?"

"Not at all. Some people are just lucky."

"Was she blackmailing you?"

Miss Creedy took a step back behind the counter. "That's ridiculous," she said shrilly.

Hamish sighed. "We believe Mrs. Gillespie was a blackmailer. If she had anything on you, I will find it out. It would be better to tell me now."

"I have led a blameless life," she shrieked. "How dare you even suggest such a thing?"

"Calm down. Now, tell me how the numbers are drawn. Is there a spinning ball with wee balls with numbers inside it?"

"No, the numbers are folded up in slips of paper by Father McNulty and then put into a large box. I just pull out the slips of paper and read the numbers."

"How many games a night?"

"Six. We break for refreshments in the middle of the evening."

"So six boxes of numbers."

"No, just the one. After each game, I give the box a good shake."

"I'll be talking to you again," said Hamish.

It could be done, he thought as he drove back. Miss Creedy could give Mrs. Gillespie a bingo card before the game. She could have two boxes. In the first might be just the numbers on Mrs. Gillespie's card. After that, the box with all the numbers would be produced.

His stomach gave a rumble, and he had a sudden longing for decent food. He called at the police station. "Won't be long," said Terry. "Nearly there."

"I'm going to the Italian place for some food. Want to come?"

"I'd rather keep on with this. You go yourself, and I'll be finished by the time you get back."

When Hamish walked into the restaurant followed by his

dog and cat, the first thing he saw was Elspeth and Luke, sitting at the table at the window.

Sonsie and Lugs slouched off to the kitchen, where they knew, from previous visits, that the Italian chef would spoil them.

Hamish felt he was being childish in not stopping at Elspeth's table to say hullo. He sat down at a table near the kitchen and as far away from them as possible. Elspeth waved to him, but he pretended not to notice.

"Your boyfriend's snubbing you," remarked Luke.

"He's not my boyfriend!"

Luke took her hand. "Then he's a silly man. What about marrying me, Elspeth?"

"Oh, sure."

"I mean it. Why not? We're both reporters. We both get on well. What about it?"

Elspeth looked amused. "How old-fashioned of you. I thought these days couples had affairs lasting, say, ten years and then decided to get married."

Elspeth glanced across at Hamish. Some imp prompted her to say, "Maybe. I'll think about it."

"'Maybe' demands a celebration. Willie!"

Willie Lamont, the waiter who had once been a police constable, came rushing up. "Champagne," said Luke.

"What's the celebration?" asked Willie.

"Miss Grant is 'maybe' going to marry me."

Hamish felt just as if a heavy wet stone had settled in his stomach.

Lucia, Willie's beautiful Italian wife, came out of the kitchen to offer her congratulations.

"It's a joke," said Elspeth desperately, but Willie arrived with the champagne.

To Luke's horror, Willie, who had given the bottle a good shake in the kitchen, opened it with a flourish and champagne sprayed all over the place.

"What do you think you're doing?" shouted Luke.

"This is what they do at Le Mans," said Willie.

"Well, this isn't Le Mans!" howled Luke, picking up a napkin and dabbing at champagne stains on his suit.

Lucia hurried off and came back with an unshaken bottle. "On the house," she said, "and I hope you will both be very happy together."

"Give the copper a glass," said Luke.

But when they looked across the restaurant, Hamish Macbeth was gone.

Hamish drove steadily towards Cnothan under a darkening sky which matched his mood. Black clouds were streaming in from the west.

It was nothing to him, nothing at all, he told himself savagely. If Elspeth wished to marry that dissipated reporter, it was her problem. His stomach gave another dismal rumble.

His cat and dog, full of food from the kitchen, slept peacefully in the back.

Cnothan was the least favourite place on his beat. He always thought of it as a sour, unwelcoming village. After a few enquiries, he found that Mrs. Forest lived in a cottage facing the dark loch, man-made by the Hydro Electric Board.

The cottage, like the others strung out along the loch, were relics of the old village, most of which had been drowned in the loch.

Hamish wondered what the previous inhabitants had been like. Maybe they had been warm-hearted and cheerful. Had many of them stayed on in the new village? How odd to think that down in the depth of the black waters were the remains of homes.

He knocked on the door of Mrs. Forest's cottage and waited. He was about to turn away when the door opened and a bent, elderly woman stared up at the tall constable. She put a liver-spotted hand to her chest, her old eyes widening with alarm.

"It's nothing serious," said Hamish soothingly. "I've just got a few wee questions to ask about Mrs. Gillespie."

"You'd best come ben."

She stood aside. Hamish walked past her. She shut the door. "To your left," she said.

Hamish walked into a low-ceilinged room. She settled herself in a chair by the fire and pointed to a chair opposite her. Hamish sat down and held his cap between his knees.

"I believe Mrs. Gillespie used to work for you."

"Only for a short time. I moved here mainly to get away from her."

"Why?"

She clasped her hands together tightly. "Do I have to tell you?"

"I will try to keep anything you tell me in confidence. She was blackmailing you, wasn't she?"

"Yes. I suppose she was."

"Please tell me what it was about."

"I was in Glasgow during the war. I got pregnant by an American serviceman. Lovely man, but he got killed in action. It was considered a sin in those days. My parents had me locked up in a hostel for unmarried mothers. My baby, a boy, was taken away for adoption, but, at that time, I was kept on in the home, doing laundry, scrubbing, things like that. It was inhumane. I escaped one day with two of the other women, and we went straight to a newspaper office and told them everything that was going on. They splashed the story, and the place was closed down. I kept the newspaper cutting, and the Gillespie woman found it. I had a wee collection of china figurines. She demanded them and said if I didn't give them to her, she would tell everyone my secret. I loved those figurines. I told her I was going to the police. She panicked and said she had just been joking. I sacked her and told her if I heard one murmur of my secret in Braikie, I *would* go to the police. She left me alone after that, but the very sight of the woman turned my stomach, so I sold up and came here. Does this need to come out?"

"No," said Hamish, "I'll make sure it doesn't. But murder is murder. I can't see you having the strength to brain her with her bucket, but have you any idea who might have done it?"

"I really don't know. But to be honest, if I did, I don't think I would tell you. She got what she deserved."

＊　　＊　　＊

When Hamish left, he wandered up the main street to a café and ordered a mutton pie and chips. Someone had left a newspaper on the table open at an article about poor diet.

He promised himself to start eating fruit and vegetables as he washed down the pie with strong tea. Then when he finished, he went back to Lochdubh, hoping there might be something in Terry's investigations to give him a clue.

Terry had left the police station, but there was a neat pile of printouts beside the computer.

Hamish gave his pets water and then settled down to read. The forensic report stated that there were no prints on the handle of the bucket: it had been wiped clean. And that was that. No tyre tracks, no hairs, no threads of cloth, nothing. He was not surprised. He remembered all the police cars arriving. He remembered pointing out the signs of a scuffle in the gravel and Blair ignoring him and walking all over the evidence with his big boots. The autopsy report was what he expected. Her death had been caused by a massive blow to the head which had crushed her skull.

As yet, there was no autopsy report on Mrs. Samson. He turned to the various interviews of the suspects. He sighed. There seemed to be nothing there more than he had found out already.

It was dark outside, and the rising wind soughed round the building. He leaned back in his chair.

At least a good picture of the late Mrs. Gillespie was beginning to emerge. The reason for her blackmailing activities was power rather than money. How she must have enjoyed getting something as simple as free cream cakes!

His thoughts moved to Elspeth. Would she really marry that reporter? Did it matter? He thought ruefully that he had had ample time in the past to propose marriage to her himself. Was he playing dog in the manger?

He switched on his answering machine. He did not expect any messages from Blair. Puffed up with the idea of a documentary on him, Blair would do anything he knew to keep him in the background. There was a brief one from Jimmy. "We don't seem to be getting anywhere with this, Hamish. Any suggestions? Found anything out?"

Then there was one from Priscilla Halburton-Smythe. "I've been reading about the murder, Hamish. I haven't heard from you in ages. How are you getting on? Give me a ring if you've got the time."

No, thought Hamish. I'm not going down that road again. I was all excited when I thought she was coming back to live here, but she only stayed for a short time and I barely saw her. He fought down that old treacherous feeling of longing. He realised the next message was from Shona Fraser.

"We're not going to go on with the documentary on Detective Chief Inspector Blair. I've been doing research on you, and I guess you acted stupid to get out of the television thing. But I've found out something interesting. I'll call at the police station at nine this evening and let you have it."

Oh, dear, thought Hamish. A Blair with fame snatched from him would be in a filthy mood and would soon be on the phone to vent some of his spleen on one local constable.

Hamish typed out a report of everything he had learned that day including his views that Mrs. Gillespie had only wanted power not money and might have contrived to win prizes at bingo by blackmailing Miss Creedy. He explained that it would account for the lack of any large sums being drawn out of the suspects' bank accounts. Then he sent it on to Jimmy.

He glanced at the clock. Seven-thirty. He took the dog and cat out for a walk and then returned to the station and took a venison stew out of the freezer and heated it up on the stove. Then he divided it equally among the three of them.

He went through to his living room and lit the fire. He switched on the television set and then surfed the channels until he found a fictional program on forensic investigation and settled down to watch. One minute he was marvelling how these forensic researchers could visit the scenes of crimes without any protective clothing whatsoever, shaking long hair and DNA all over the place and trudging around dead bodies in uncovered shoes, when he fell asleep.

He woke abruptly and looked at his watch. Ten o'clock. He wondered if Shona had called and he hadn't heard her. But he knew that in the past no matter how heavily he slept, a knock at the door always awoke him.

He stretched and yawned. Maybe she had changed her mind.

Archie Maclean, the fisherman, swallowed the last of a cup of extremely strong tea and went up on deck. He was wearing a tracksuit under his oilskin. He kept clothes on board, for he knew his bullying wife expected him to go to sea in his suit and collar and tie. "You're the skipper," she always said, "and should look the part."

His boat, the *Sally Jane*, bucketed through the increasingly high waves as she headed out from the loch towards the Atlantic. The earlier clouds which had threatened rain had disappeared, and a full moon rode the skies.

They were nearly at the entrance to the loch when Archie, who was about to go up to the wheelhouse and take over, spotted a rowing boat cresting a wave. Why it had not been overturned was a miracle. He nipped up to the wheelhouse and said to his mate, Harry, "There's a wee rowboat in the water. Pull her ower and let's have a look."

Harry reduced the speed. Archie unhitched a pair of binoculars and then let out a hiss of alarm. "There iss some cheil lying in the boat. Pull alongside."

He ran back to the rail and called to the other three men who made up his small crew. "Get a grappling iron and pull her in."

It was a difficult job with the waves heaving the *Sally Jane* up and down. "Bring a light," shouted Archie.

A grappling iron was attached to the rowing boat. Archie shone a powerful torch down into it. A young girl lay sprawled in the bottom facedown.

"Bang goes a night's fishing," said Archie. "There's blood on the back o' her head. I'll phone Macbeth."

Hamish Macbeth stood on the harbour, waiting for the fishing boat to come in. In the distance, he could hear police sirens. He was wearing the blue forensic suit all police officers were now expected to wear when inspecting a crime. He felt guilty about it. He had worn it when he had been cleaning out the hen run on a wet day. It had subsequently fallen off a hook on the back of the kitchen door, and Sonsie had slept on it.

He thought miserably of forensic programmes he had watched on television. "Ah, I have one hair here!" some forensic scientist would say triumphantly. God only knew what they would find if they ever took away his protective clothing for examination.

The sirens sounded nearer. Lights were going on in the cottages along the waterfront.

Elspeth woke up suddenly in her room at the hotel. She heard the wail of the sirens as police cars sped past and down the hill to Lochdubh. She went out of her room and hammered on the door of Luke's room.

He opened it and stood looking blearily down at her. His eyes were bloodshot, and he smelled strongly of booze.

"I've heard lots of police cars going past," said Elspeth. "Come on. Get dressed!"

Luke groaned. After an unsuccessful evening trying to get Elspeth into his bed, he had resorted to comfort from a bottle of whisky.

"You go," he said. "I'll follow you down."

"We've only got the one car!"

"I'll wake someone up and take one of the hotel cars."

Luke retreated into his room and shut the door. Just five minutes more sleep, he thought. He fell facedown on the bed, not waking until the morning.

*   *   *

The fishing boat came nearer. Jimmy shivered. "Did Archie say who it was?" he asked Hamish.

"He chust said a wee lassie. Oh, God, Jimmy, I chust hope it isnae who I think it is."

"That being?"

"Shona Fraser. She phoned earlier and said she had something to tell me. She said she would come to the police station, but she never arrived."

A woman police inspector was waiting, flanked by a woman police sergeant.

"Look at them," said Jimmy. "It's all this political correctness. The whole Northern Constabulary will soon be filled with damn women."

"If it iss Shona," muttered Hamish, "what could she have found out that I couldn't?"

"Beats me. Amazing if it wasn't Blair who killed her. He was flaming mad when he was told that the television documentary was cancelled."

"Where is the auld scunner?"

"Probably nursing a hangover. Here comes trouble!"

Hamish walked forward. "You! Macbeth!" barked Police Inspector Mary Gannon. "Go and knock on doors and see if anyone heard anything."

Hamish trudged off. The pity of it was, he thought, that the hotel on the harbour had been boarded for years. The pub beside it still closed at eleven o'clock in the evening. There was no cottage looking directly onto the harbour.

The lights were on in Patel's store. Patel was the epitome of the Indian businessman. He knew that crowds of people even in the middle of the night meant a good sale of sandwiches and hot coffee.

Hamish pushed open the door and went in. Mr. Patel was just carrying a plate of sandwiches through from the kitchen at the back.

"What's going on, Hamish?"

"A dead body in a rowing boat. Archie caught it when he was out at the fishing. Did you see anyone at all? I would guess down by the harbour or approaching the police station. It's a young lassie. I can't see anyone going to the trouble of putting a dead body in a rowing boat and floating it out to sea. My guess is that the girl was hit from behind with a hard enough blow to kill her. Then she was toppled over the sea wall but fell into one of the rowing boats. The murderer went down the stairs but maybe heard someone coming and slashed the painter so that the boat drifted off. The tide would be on the turn."

"I didnae see anyone, Hamish. Coffee? I've made some fresh."

"No, I'd better get on with it."

Hamish opened the shop door and looked outside. Mary Gannon believed in blanket coverage. Policemen were knocking at doors all along the waterfront.

Where was Shona's car? That is, if the dead girl was Shona.

Then he recognised it. It was parked a little away from the police station. His heart sank. Had he been so heavily asleep that he had not heard her knock?

He took out his torch because the car was parked between

two street lights and in the shadow. He shone the torch around it and then saw a tyre iron lying on the ground.

Hamish picked it up gingerly with one gloved hand and walked over to where Mary Gannon was directing operations.

"I found this, ma'am," said Hamish. "There's blood on the end of it, and I think this is the murder weapon. I found it beside that television researcher Shona Fraser's car. She left me a message saying she was going to call on me this evening because she had some information for me. Shona Fraser was supposed to be doing research for a documentary on Detective Chief Inspector Blair. Oh, here comes Mr. Blair."

"Go over to the forensics' van and get yourself an evidence bag and seal this and mark it."

"Yes, ma'am."

As Hamish moved off, he heard Blair saying, "I'm in charge here."

Then came Mary's frosty reply: "Everything is in hand."

Blair: "This is a job for detectives, and you aren't a detective."

Mary: "Are you questioning my ability?"

Blair: "Och, no, sweetheart. Just you run along and get a cup of tea or something."

Mary: "Don't patronise me!"

Blair: "Look here, you boot-faced bag. You'll stop getting your knickers in a twist and do what you're told. God help the force the day the beaver patrol takes over."

Mary swung round to her listening sergeant. "You've heard all of this? Then type up a report, and I will deliver it to Superintendent Daviot in the morning."

Hamish, almost out of earshot, could hear the frightened Blair beginning to wheedle and beg.

After he had delivered the tyre iron and was heading back, he found himself confronted by Elspeth.

"What's happened, Hamish?"

"I cannae tell you wi' all my masters looking on. Over there, that woman is Police Inspector Gannon. You'll need to ask her."

Hamish went back to the car and began to search around it again. Then he shone his torch inside. A handbag was lying on the passenger seat.

Mary Gannon came up behind him.

"Her car?"

"Yes."

"See if it's locked."

Hamish tried the handle on the passenger side, and the door opened. "Her keys are still in the ignition," he said.

"Bring that handbag into the police station, and we'll look through it. I'll tell forensics to tow this car away for examination. I will join you shortly. Don't open the bag until I am there."

Hamish went into the police station. He stripped off the forensic suit, hung it on a peg behind the door, and lit the stove. He boiled up water for coffee and put sugar, milk, two cups, and a plate of shortbread on the table.

The kitchen door opened just after he had made the coffee, and Mary walked in. If it hadn't been for her stern features, she would have appeared a motherly woman. She had a full face and brown eyes. Her figure was matronly. She took off her hat and rubbed her eyes. "Gosh, I'm tired."

"Coffee?"

"Yes, just black."

Then Hamish realised Mary's eyes were widening, and she was reaching for the canister of CS gas on her belt. He swung round. Sonsie was crouched there, staring out of yellow eyes.

"Don't!" he yelled. "It's my cat. Sonsie, go back to bed."

The cat slouched off.

"That's a wild cat," said Mary accusingly.

"It's very domesticated," said Hamish soothingly. "Besides, they're all hybrids now. I doubt if you could find a genuine wild cat in the Highlands."

Lugs pattered in, looked up at Mary out of his odd blue eyes, and walked out again.

"Do you have a whole menagerie in this police station?"

"No, no," said Hamish, pouring coffee. "Just the two beasts."

"Right, let's get down to business. May I have a piece of shortbread?"

"Go ahead."

Mary tried to take a bite. "This is made of bricks."

Hamish flushed. "It wass made by my friend Mrs. Brodie. Herself iss not very good in the cooking department."

"Okay. We need fresh gloves." Hamish went through to a cupboard in the office and came back with a packet of latex gloves.

They both put on a pair, and Mary opened the handbag. "Get some clean paper, and I'll tip this lot out."

Hamish came back with sheets of computer printing paper. Mary gently turned the contents out onto the paper.

There was the usual clutter one would find in any woman's handbag: house keys, wallet, driving licence, two pens, comb, lipstick, strong mints, a packet of tissues, address book and notebook, one earring, and an invitation to the opening of a new restaurant in Strathbane.

Mary looked at the driving licence. "Yes, it's Shona Fraser. You look at the address book, and I'll look at the notebook. Lock the door first."

Hamish raised an eyebrow. "I don't want to be interrupted," she said. "Do it!"

Hamish locked the door and returned to the table. "This is in shorthand," complained Mary. "I have speed writing, but I can't read shorthand."

"I'll read it," said Hamish.

He quickly scanned through the contents. At first, there were enthusiastic notes about the proposed documentary and then comments such as "I don't think Macbeth is as stupid as he would like me to think. But Blair, now, is stupid."

Hamish flipped to the end. "I decided to go and see some of the suspects on my own just to see if we could do a documentary on the murder. I couldn't believe it. Got to see Macbeth . . . ," Hamish read. "That's the last item. She must have been struck down when she got out of the car. She was a little thing. She was dragged across to the sea wall and tipped over. But it was high tide, and three rowing boats which are tied up just under that bit opposite where her car was parked would be afloat. The body lands in one of them. Our murderer goes down the steps but hears some noise above and, frightened of being discovered with a dead body, cuts the painter and pushes the boat out to sea. If Archie hadn't spotted it, the boat would have gone out to the Atlantic on the receding tide, been tipped over, and the body might not have been found."

A sudden hammering at the door made Hamish jump. Then they heard Blair's voice. "If you're in there, you lazy hound, get out here!"

They sat in silence until they could hear him retreating.

"You know," said Mary thoughtfully, studying Hamish, "I've heard a lot of stories about you, how you didn't want promotion and all that. I didn't believe it. Everyone is ambitious. But I can see what you mean now. My husband's business is doing well, and there's no need for me to work. I listen to Blair yapping, and I think, I don't need this. No more being dragged out of bed in the middle of the night with a phone call. No more nasty remarks against women in the police force. No more horrible surprises dumped in my locker. I'll see this case through, and then I'm off.

"I'd better get back to the scene and give this to the forensic boys. Have you an evidence bag?"

Hamish nodded. He went to the office and brought a large one back. Mary put the address book and notebook in the handbag, and Hamish sealed it up.

"Mrs. Gillespie is being buried at eleven o'clock today," said Mary, getting to her feet. "I suggest you attend the funeral. It's at St. Mary's. See who turns up, and then I would like you to get into plain clothes and something to cover that red hair of yours and keep a watch on the professor. See what he does and where he goes. Leave it to the afternoon because he'll be interviewed in the morning. Police and detectives will interview the other suspects. We'll get onto this Creedy woman you mentioned in your notes and see if we can get her to confess she rigged the bingo. I managed to pick up a copy of your notes tonight before I left headquarters and read them on the road over. Get some sleep. I'll tell Blair I sent you off somewhere."

Hamish let her out and locked the door again behind her. If only someone like that had Blair's job, he thought before taking himself off to bed.

Chapter Seven

If you want to win her hand,
Let the maiden understand
That she's not the only pebble on the beach.

—Harry Braisted

Hamish thought that the day of the funeral for such as Mavis Gillespie should be black and ominous. But the sun shone and the birds twittered in the trees surrounding St. Mary's. Heather, her daughter, was there with her father. That was the sum total of the mourners. There was not even one elderly soul of the kind who loved to attend funerals in the church.

Father McNulty did his best. Hamish, Heather, and Mr. Gillespie sang the hymns and listened dry-eyed to the service. Then they followed the coffin to the public cemetery, where the body was interred.

"That's that," said Heather. "Now we can get on with our lives. Come along, Dad."

"A moment of your time," said Hamish. "Are you sure

neither of you have any idea who might have killed Mrs. Gillespie?"

"I can't think of anyone," said Heather. "I'll need to get Dad home. He's not well."

Hamish went back to the police station, in front of which a mobile police unit had been set up. Television crews and reporters were everywhere. Avoiding questions, he went into the station and changed into a sweater and jeans and pulled a black wool cap over his hair.

Then, running the barrage of press questions again, he got into his Land Rover and headed to Angela Brodie's home.

"What is it, Hamish?" she asked.

"I've two favours to ask. May I borrow your car? I've got to follow someone, and I can't do it in a police vehicle."

"All right. I'm not going anywhere today. That poor little girl! What an awful thing to happen. I've been interviewed five times since last night. The whole thing is so badly coordinated. What's the other favour? Oh, I know. That dog and cat of yours."

"You don't need to take them in," wheedled Hamish. "I've left food for them on the kitchen table, and all you need to do is feed them and let them out for a walk."

"Hamish!"

"I know, I know. But when this case is over, you'll never need to see them."

"This is the last time."

"Okay, Angela. I'm off."

"Wait! You forgot my car keys."

*　*　*

Hamish parked Angela's small Ford Escort at the end of the cul-de-sac where the professor had his house, and waited. He wondered whether the inspector really hoped he would find something out or whether she was smarter than Blair at getting him out of the case. And did she realise how hard it was to tail someone on usually empty highland roads?

The morning wore on. Hamish had packed a flask of coffee and a packet of chicken sandwiches and was just thinking about getting out an early lunch when the professor's car backed out of his driveway.

Hamish waited until he had driven past, then eased out and followed him as far back as he could without losing sight of the professor.

Professor Sander parked in the main street and got out. Hamish parked between two other cars and watched. The professor went into the butchers and emerged holding a carrier bag. Then he went into the greengrocers. Hamish waited glumly while the professor did his shopping, going from shop to shop. When he stowed his groceries in his car and moved off, Hamish followed. Back to his home went the professor.

Hamish parked again at the edge of the cul-de-sac. He moodily drank coffee and munched sandwiches and waited.

It was a rare fine day with little wisps of cloud drifting across a pale blue sky. He began to feel sleepy. He hadn't had much sleep the night before. His eyelids drooped. He let out a gentle snore. He drifted into a dream of chasing a black figure up and over the heather. He was just gaining on the anonymous figure when it turned around, revealing the face of Detective Chief Inspector Blair.

Hamish awoke with a jerk. Had he missed the professor? He climbed stiffly out of Angela's small car and walked along the cul-de-sac. The professor's car was not in the drive.

Hamish raced back to the car and drove into Braikie, scanning the parked cars as he went along. He drove out of Braikie. The professor's car was a black BMW. He came to the crossroads where one road led to Strathbane and the other to Lochdubh. He took the Strathbane road.

He drove quickly, the twisting road in front of him so far empty of any other vehicle.

He topped the rise where a long, straight stretch of road led down from the hills and into Strathbane, and in the distance he saw a black car. He raced the car up to ninety, hoping it would stand the strain.

He put on the brakes just as the thirty-mile-an-hour speed restriction loomed up. He now recognised the BMW ahead.

He followed carefully, glad of the town's increased traffic. The professor drove to the multi-storey car park in the centre. Hamish followed. The professor parked. Hamish parked a little way away and then, getting out, followed at a discreet distance.

He had a sinking feeling that Professor Sander had come to Strathbane for no other reason than more shopping.

They were on the fourth floor of the car park. The professor walked to the lift. Hamish took the stairs and waited outside the car park.

The professor emerged and Hamish followed. First the professor went to a large bookshop and spent a considerable amount of time inside. When he finally emerged carrying a plastic bag full of books, he headed straight back for the car park.

No, thought Hamish, I am not going to follow him all the way back to Braikie. What a waste of time! He suddenly wanted food, and good food at that.

He saw a small French restaurant and decided to eat there. Occasionally good restaurants would spring up in Strathbane, only to close down after a few months, defeated by the local population's desire for nothing other than junk food.

He glanced at his watch. Seven in the evening. He pushed open the door and went in. The restaurant was divided into booths, separated from each other by wooden partitions topped with curtained brass rails.

The prices made him blink, but there was a set menu for twenty pounds. He chose lobster bisque, followed by sea bream and salad, and although he would have liked some wine, he decided to settle for mineral water instead.

"I can't go on like this," said a woman's voice in the booth behind him. "People are talking. Why don't you get a divorce?"

Hamish, who had been about to remove his wool hat, pulled it further down about his ears instead. He recognised that voice. It was Fiona Fleming.

"I can't." Male voice: Dr. Renfrew. "I have my position in the community to consider. Look, it's been fun, but let's just leave it now. People are beginning to talk."

"I'll tell your wife, you bastard. You can't dump me just like that. You said you wanted to spend the rest of your life with me!"

"Men say a lot of things in the . . . er . . . heat of the moment that they don't mean. Look, Fiona, darling, we can still be friends."

Ouch, thought Hamish. He's for it now.

There came a splashing sound, and then the top of Fiona's head appeared above the partition. Must have thrown her drink over him, Hamish guessed.

"I'll make you sorry. I'll make you wish you'd never been born," howled Fiona.

No one ever says anything original when they're hurt, thought Hamish.

Then came the sound of rapidly retreating high heels.

He heard the doctor calling for the bill.

If she did kill her husband, thought Hamish, that man's life will be in danger. Even if she didn't, I think she'll turn really vicious.

He concentrated on eating his meal, wondering what to do next. Would Inspector Gannon really expect him to go on following the professor, day in and day out?

Hamish finished his meal and returned to Lochdubh. Television vans were drawn up along the waterfront. He prayed some other big story would break and take them all away.

Jimmy Anderson had seen him arrive and hurried over to the police station to join him.

"So what's the latest?" asked Hamish.

"Shona was struck down with a tyre iron. Dumped in the boat. Pushed out to sea."

"And no one saw anything?"

"Oh, they all saw something or heard something, but that was because of the bloody television cameras. Even those

Currie sisters were wearing make-up and inventing things like mad."

"How do you know they were inventing things?"

"I'm apt to discount reports of a tall black man with a scar."

"Oh, dear. Still, I'd like to go through them just in case. There might be something there. Any report on the bank balances?"

"Nothing important, fifty pounds here, a couple of hundred there."

They were standing together outside the police station. Hamish saw Mary Gannon approaching them from the police mobile unit.

"Well, Macbeth, anything to report?"

"No, ma'am. He shopped in Braikie, and then he went to Strathbane and bought books and went back home. But I was in a restaurant in Strathbane and I overheard Dr. Renfrew, who has been having an affair, telling Fiona Fleming that it was all over, and she threatened to make him sorry."

"Write a report of that and let me have it. Was the professor in this restaurant?"

"No, ma'am."

"Then what were you doing in the restaurant?"

"It was obvious the professor was going back home, and I was hungry."

"You were told to follow him, not disobey orders because you were hungry. Get back on it tomorrow. He's our strongest lead."

She turned on her heel and walked away. Mary had received

a stern warning from Daviot not to get too friendly with Hamish, due to a spiteful report from Blair.

"Michty me!" said Hamish. "Didn't anyone ask the professor what he was doing when Shona was getting bashed on the head?"

"I did. Got him up at dawn. Was he furious! Said he was in his bed fast asleep. No alibi, as he lives alone. Same with the rest of them."

"It's getting late and I'm tired," said Hamish. "I am not going to hang around here, or she'll find something to keep me up all night."

"Now what?" asked the manager of the Tommel Castle Hotel when Hamish arrived carrying an overnight bag and followed by his cat and dog.

"I really need a quiet night," pleaded Hamish, "and I'm not going to get it if I stay at the police station."

"Oh, all right. I can let you have a spare room, but that's all you get. Leave the minibar alone, and breakfast is not included in this non-paying visit."

Elspeth was sitting in the bar with Luke when she saw Hamish arrive and then follow Mr. Johnson up the stairs.

"Back in a minute," she said to Luke. He barely heard her. He was surrounded by other reporters, and all were busy making up legends about each other. Luke had not repeated his proposal of marriage, and Elspeth assumed he had proffered it because he wanted to tease Hamish. He made a few desultory tries to make love to her which she always rebuffed.

Hamish was just unpacking his bag when Elspeth knocked on his door.

"Oh, it's you," he said bleakly. "I was just going to bed. What do you want?"

"I want to talk about the murders."

"Look, I've got a dragon of a police inspector on my back, and I can't talk to the press."

"I wanted to talk as friends."

Hamish looked down at the small figure of Elspeth. She was casually dressed in a white Aran sweater, jeans, and smart black leather boots. Her odd silver eyes studied his face.

"All right," said Hamish, suddenly remembering how useful Elspeth's intuition had been in the past. "I can't offer you a drink because the room's free and I've been told not to touch the minibar."

"Fine. I see Lugs and Sonsie have made themselves comfortable on the bed. I hope there's room for you."

"I'll just push them to one side."

There were two easy chairs in front of the window. They both sat down.

"Go ahead," said Elspeth. "It's all off the record."

"Not a word to Luke!"

"Promise."

Hamish outlined everything he knew. When he finished, Elspeth sat very still. Then she said, "Wouldn't it be odd if we had two murderers here?"

"How do you mean?"

"Say Professor Sander did pinch that student's work. He's a very vain man. I can see him following Mrs. Gillespie down his drive, and overcome with rage, braining her with her bucket. Or Fiona Fleming might really have pushed her husband down the stairs, although I doubt it, and decided to get rid of Mrs. Gillespie once and for all."

"But what about Shona Fraser?"

"Ah, I'm coming to that. Before she came up here, Shona Fraser worked in London for Trant TV. She worked as a researcher. Now, Trant TV specialises in reality television—you know, fly-on-the wall documentaries, exposures of famous people. They did a scam with that soap actress Bernice James. One of their reporters pretended to be a drug dealer and went to her hotel room to supply her with coke. They had a hidden camera and got her snorting coke on film. What if Shona had found out something about someone during her researches and they followed her up here and killed her to keep her quiet?"

"How do you know all this about Shona?"

"From the London press in the bar. You may not like the press, Hamish, but they sometimes can find out things the police can't."

"How long was Shona working for Trant TV?"

"I don't know. I can easily find out. So can you."

"It's hard for me to get a bit of peace from my superiors these days. Could you . . . ?"

"Very well. How can I contact you?"

"I'll give you my mobile phone number. Is there anything serious between you and Luke?"

Elspeth hesitated. Then she decided it would be better to leave Hamish guessing. He had hurt her badly in the past, and she had no intention of letting him hurt her again.

"Mind your own business," she said. "Any news of darling Priscilla?"

Hamish flushed angrily. "I don't want to talk about it."

Sonsie let out a slow hiss.

"I'd better go," said Elspeth. "Your guard cat is getting upset."

"Look, I'm very grateful to you for this stuff about Shona. There may well be something there. I've got to follow the professor again tomorrow. I feel it's a waste of time."

Elspeth had half risen. She sat down again. "I've a thought. What about Miss Creedy?"

"She may well have been fiddling the bingo results—but murder!"

"There are still people in this wicked world today who prize respectability, particularly in small towns and villages."

"But Mrs. Gillespie couldn't have threatened to expose her without exposing herself."

"Look at it another way. She must have had something on Miss Creedy to make the woman even want to cheat."

Hamish groaned. "I only wish I wasn't stuck with the professor."

"I really am off now, Hamish." Elspeth stood up, and Hamish followed her to the door. "I tell you what, I might have a go at Miss Creedy myself."

"Would you? That would be grand. I'll buy you dinner tomorrow night."

"Oh yeah, Sherlock? And like those previous times, you'll fail to turn up."

"I'm sorry about that. If I could just explain . . ."

"Forget it. I'll call you tomorrow."

✳   ✳   ✳

Hamish showered and got into his pyjamas, lifted his grumbling pets off the bed, and got in himself. The cat leapt back on and lay beside him, and Lugs lay at his feet. He fell into a dreamless sleep, not waking until seven in the morning.

Hamish left his pets at the police station and was getting into the Land Rover again when Mary Gannon came up behind him, making him jump.

Hamish swung round. "Just off to Braikie," he said.

"See you keep on the job. Do not speak to the press. I know you show great insight and intelligence, but it is necessary in a big case like this that we all work together, and that means following orders. Do you understand me?"

"Yes, ma'am."

"That's the stuff," said Blair, coming up to join them. "That laddie needs a wumman's firm touch."

"Mr. Blair, if I want your advice, I'll ask for it," snapped Mary.

"Och, come on. It was just a wee joke. The way you females take on."

"Any more of that, and I'll have you up before the board for sexual discrimination. Also for alcoholism. You stink of booze and at this time in the morning!"

Hamish got into Angela's car and sped off, leaving them to it.

It was one of those grey misty days in the Highlands where all the colour is bleached out of the landscape and sounds are muffled. The mist grew thicker as he reached Braikie and parked at the end of the cul-de-sac.

It was one of the few times when he regretted remaining a mere policeman. He was out of the loop, away from recent discoveries and statements from the suspects. Maybe he should have told the inspector about the possibility Shona had found out something about one of the suspects when she was working in London, but Mary would ask how he had come about such information and then would give him a row for discussing the case with a member of the hated press.

He was just bemoaning the fact that he had forgotten to bring coffee and sandwiches with him when a police car drew alongside. He rolled down the window.

"Driving licence and papers," snapped one, "and get out of the car."

Hamish uncoiled his length from Angela's small car and pulled his police card out of his pocket, saying as he did so, "I'm PC Hamish Macbeth from Lochdubh. I'm here to watch the professor. Instructions from Inspector Gannon. What's up?"

"The neighbours have been complaining about a sinister-looking man—that's you—casing the houses."

God bless them all, thought Hamish. He phoned headquarters and got patched through to Mary's phone. When he finished explaining, she said impatiently, "It's your fault for making yourself so obvious."

"It's hard not to be obvious in a highland town," protested Hamish.

"You'd better leave it. Get back and put your uniform on

and go over to Styre. Mrs. Barret-Wilkinson was not available when we called. Find out where she was the night before last."

Back to the police station, into uniform, picnic basket loaded up with people food and animal food, and off in the Land Rover with the dog and cat. Hamish whistled cheerfully. He was glad to get out of what had looked like a long and boring day.

As he mounted the crest of the hill above Lochdubh, the mist rolled up the mountain sides, and soon the sun shone out. The landscape was a blaze of colour: yellow broom, purple heather, and rowan berries as red as blood.

Mrs. Barret-Wilkinson was not at home. Her car was gone. Hamish drove down to the beach and let the dog and cat out. He unpacked the picnic basket, spread a rug on the beach, and ate a leisurely brunch after feeding Lugs and Sonsie.

The sea was calm with sunlight rippling on tiny waves plashing gently on the shingly beach. The air smelled of salt and peat smoke. From one of the little cottages of Styre came the sounds of a football match on the radio.

How far it all was from the bustle and grime of the cities and the miseries of murder, thought Hamish. But unless the murders were solved, a dark stain of suspicion and dread would be left.

Back to work. He packed everything up with a sigh. Time to see if Mrs. Barret-Wilkinson had returned.

When he went back to her house, he was in time to see her

getting out of her car. She took a large suitcase out of the boot. Hamish approached her.

"What now?" she asked.

"Do you know a television researcher called Shona Fraser was murdered in Lochdubh two nights ago?"

"Yes, I heard it on the radio when I was driving north. What's it got to do with me?"

"I have to take a statement from you," said Hamish soothingly. "Where were you the night before last?"

"I was visiting a friend in Glasgow."

"I'll need the name and address."

She sighed. "Come into the house, and I'll write it down for you."

Hamish followed her into the faux country house living room.

She went to a desk and wrote on a pad of paper and then tore a sheet off. "There you are. Bella will confirm that I was with her the night before last. And last night, I stopped at the Palace Hotel in Inverness." She opened her handbag and took out a receipt. "There is my hotel receipt. Now, I'd like to get on with unpacking."

That was that, he thought. He'd phone over the details, and Strathclyde police would check her alibi.

"Just one thing," said Hamish. "Why did you choose to live in an isolated place like this?"

"I wanted a quiet life. I like it here. I could afford a house this size in such a remote place where I could not afford it in the city. Now, if you don't mind . . ."

Hamish decided to drive to Lochdubh with this information rather than phone it over. That way, he might find out what else was going on.

He was climbing into the Land Rover when his phone rang. It was Elspeth.

"Good news, Hamish. Shona was working on the background of doctors who had been sued for malpractice, and one of the subjects was Dr. Renfrew. He had told a woman that the rash on her breast was merely caused by an allergy to her bra. He prescribed ointments. This went on for months. It got worse. By the time the woman decided to get a second opinion, it was found she had invasive cancer and it was well advanced. The fact that she didn't lose her life was a miracle, but she sued Dr. Renfrew for malpractice. He was not struck off the medical register and he was heavily insured against malpractice suits, so he got away with it. He wouldn't give an interview, but there were television shots of him leaving his house and shouting at the reporter. He came up to Braikie Hospital last year."

"Elspeth, I'll go and talk to him. If I phone this in, they'll send a detective and I'll end up never getting an idea of who was guilty."

So Hamish phoned over a report of Mrs. Barret-Wilkinson's alibi to the mobile police unit, saying he would type it up and deliver it later with the receipt.

The policeman who answered the phone said, "Wait a minute. The inspector's just coming."

"Talk to her later," said Hamish, and rang off.

Now for Dr. Renfrew.

*   *   *

At the hospital, he was told it was Dr. Renfrew's day off. He got his address, which was some way out of Braikie.

The doctor's home was a square Scottish Georgian house, a relic of the days when army officers were quartered in the Highlands after the Battle of Culloden.

It looked a dark forbidding sort of place, and the garden was unkempt with a small square of shaggy lawn and straggly bushes.

He rang the doorbell. It was answered by a harassed-looking woman.

"What is it?" she asked.

"Mrs. Renfrew?"

"Yes."

"Is your husband at home?"

"Is this necessary? He's already been interviewed by the police."

"Something else has come up. I would really like to speak to him."

"Don't be long about it."

She turned away, and Hamish followed her into a dark, stone-flagged hall. She pushed open a door and said, "Darling, it's the police again."

Dr. Renfrew was sitting in an armchair beside a smouldering fire. The day had turned warm, but the house was cold.

The doctor threw down the newspaper he had been reading and got angrily to his feet. "This is too much. I shall put in a complaint."

Hamish turned round. Mrs. Renfrew was standing in the doorway.

"I think it would be better if we were alone, Dr. Renfrew."

He hesitated only a moment and then said, "Elsie, go and do something or other and shut the door behind you."

Elsie shut the door with unnecessary force.

"So what is it now?" demanded Dr. Renfrew. "I have already been asked to account for my movements the night that researcher was murdered, which, I may add, I consider the highest degree of impertinence."

"Did you tell the police you had met Shona Fraser before?"

"What!"

"When she was working as a researcher for a London-based television company, she must have interviewed you for their programme on medical malpractice."

His face turned a muddy colour. "I never saw her. Yes, they tried to interview me, but I either refused to answer the door or ran past them when I left the house or surgery. It was a genuine mistake. It's all over now."

"Except," said Hamish slowly, "when Mrs. Gillespie recognised you from the programme and blackmailed you. What did she want?"

All the bluster had gone out of Dr. Renfrew. He said in a low voice, "A bit of money, here and there, not much. And drugs."

"Drugs!" exclaimed Hamish. What was happening in the Highlands, he marvelled, when middle-aged charwomen turned out to be drug addicts? "What was it? Cocaine? Heroin?"

He gave a bleak smile. "No, nothing like that. Hyperex."

"What on earth is Hyperex?"

"She had osteoarthritis. Hyperex was a drug for sufferers,

but it was considered dangerous and we were told to withdraw all supplies. But we still had some at the hospital. She insisted it was the only thing that helped and said if I didn't give it to her she would broadcast my malpractice suit all over Braikie. I'm glad she's dead, but I didn't kill her."

"I'm sorry," said Hamish. "But I'll need to ask you to come with me to make a statement."

He looked completely defeated. "I'll get my jacket," he said.

At the mobile police unit, Blair was nowhere in sight, but Inspector Gannon was there. Hamish briefly explained what he had found out, not mentioning Elspeth's name but saying instead that he had remembered seeing the documentary on television.

"Good work," she said. "There's been a burglary at a croft on the Strathbane road. It's just come in. I want you to get over there and do the initial interview, and I'll send along some fingerprint men if we can spare them. Here's the address. Off you go while I get down to getting a statement from the doctor."

Hamish opened his mouth to protest and then shut it again, quickly deciding any protest would be futile. But he felt very angry with her. He had given her the first real breakthrough in the case, and he was being sidetracked. They could easily have sent out a policeman from Strathbane.

He walked to his Land Rover and looked at the name and address. Geordie McArthur, The Sheiling, Strathbane Road. It was several months since he had called on Geordie. He liked to occasionally check up on people in the outlying crofts.

*   *   *

As he approached, Hamish reflected it was a typical croft house. Outside were two rusting cars, an old television set, and a fridge.

Other people might decorate the outside of their houses with flower gardens, but your true crofter used it as a dump for discarded machinery and household goods in the dim hope that some bits might come in handy some day.

Geordie's wife, a thin, leathery woman with a face set in perpetual lines of discontent, invited him in. She said Geordie was asleep and went to wake him.

Sutherland boasts some of the tallest men in the British Isles. Geordie's head scraped the low ceiling when he came into the living room.

"So what was taken, Geordie?" asked Hamish.

"My Land Rover. Two nights ago."

"And you've only got around to reporting it now! I'll need the registration number and a description."

"You can see for yourself. It's parked round the back of the house."

"Geordie. This is right daft. It's been stolen or it hasn't been stolen."

"Look, I havenae used it for three days, right? Well, I checked the mileage, and there were miles on it that werenae there before. I always check the mileage because herself sometimes takes it out when I'm asleep."

"Why shouldn't she?" asked Hamish.

"I don't want herself flitting off tae Strathbane to flaunt herself in front of other men."

Hamish stared at the big man in amazement. Did he really see his downtrodden, weather-beaten wife as such an object of desire?

"Let's see the Land Rover, Geordie."

Geordie led the way round the back of the croft house to where the Land Rover was parked. There's a full-blown murder case going on, Hamish thought, and here am I stuck with this loon.

"See," said Geordie, "I leave the keys in it." He opened the driver's door. "I've got this wee book. I aye take a note of the mileage. Well, it had gained twenty miles. What's up with you, man? You look like you've been struck by the lightning."

For Hamish was suddenly standing stock-still, his eyes vague and his mouth open.

"Give me a minute, Geordie," he said.

Hamish looked down the fields to the Strathbane road. Twenty miles would cover the round trip to Lochdubh. Could someone who didn't want their car recognised have stolen the Land Rover for the sole purpose of killing Shona Fraser?

"Are you sure it wasn't your wife?"

"Sure as sure. I keep an eye on her."

Hamish thought, I'll need to come back when this is all over and see what I can do for Mrs. McArthur.

"There's another thing," said Geordie. "Whoever took it gave it a fair cleaning."

"Right," said Hamish. "Stand away from it now, Geordie, and don't touch it again. I'll get a forensic team out."

"I neffer thought you'd take it this serious."

Hamish phoned and got through to Inspector Gannon by

saying it was urgent and in connection with the murder of Shona. She listened to him and said she would send a forensic team out right away.

Hamish did not ask her for further instructions. He wanted time to think.

Chapter Eight

I do not mind lying, but I hate inaccuracy.

—Samuel Butler

Hamish waited patiently for the forensic team to arrive. Geordie lit a cigarette, and Hamish sniffed the air longingly. He wondered if the occasional craving for a cigarette would ever leave him.

"Geordie," he said, "I was going to leave this until later, but I'll need to have a wee talk with you about the treatment of your wife."

"Whit!"

"As far as I can see, you keep her a sort of prisoner. Why shouldn't she take the car and go shopping if she feels like it?"

"She'll meet ither men. She'll waste my money on baubles."

"Church-goer, are you?" asked Hamish.

"I am a staunch member of the Free Presbyterians."

"I might have thought you a member of the Taliban. Your

wife's a decent middle-aged woman. The way you've ruined her looks is enough to put any man off."

"What are you talking about? I treat that woman fair and decent. She gets three meals a day."

"You're out o' the Dark Ages, that's what you are," said Hamish bitterly. "And you need some sort of therapy. I'll be having a word with your minister."

"Be damned to ye! Ye are an emissary of Satan." Geordie swung a punch at Hamish, who dodged it neatly.

"Try that again," said Hamish, "and I'll arrest you for assaulting a police officer. I'm telling you, Geordie, you've been stuck up here for so long wi' nothing but your sheep and that poor wife of yours and it's fair turned your brain. Here come the forensics."

Mary was with them. As they got to work, she looked suspiciously at Hamish. "I don't trust you, Macbeth," she said. "I think you are holding back information."

"Why?"

"I don't believe in coincidence. You happen to be in a restaurant in Strathbane when Dr. Renfrew and Mrs. Fleming are having a row. You happen suddenly to remember a television programme on malpractice, and now you suddenly discover that this man's Land Rover could have been driven on the night of Shona Fraser's murder."

"I didnae know anything about this Land Rover. You told me there had been a burglary and sent me off to investigate," said Hamish.

"Maybe you're just lucky. Get along with you. Write up

your reports at the police station and leave them for me at the mobile unit."

"Yes, ma'am." Hamish touched his cap and headed off to his own vehicle.

As he was driving into Lochdubh, he saw the long, low Presbyterian church and stopped abruptly. The minister's house was at the side of it, a modern bungalow with plaster gnomes in the garden. Hamish wondered why plaster gnomes were not considered too frivolous.

The door was opened by a pretty young woman. She had rosy cheeks and a mop of glossy brown curls.

"I saw you admiring the gnomes," she said cheerfully. "Aren't they awful? One of the parishioners gave them to Murdo, so we have to display them. You're Hamish Macbeth. We met last year at Jaunty Sinclair's wedding."

"Of course! You're the minister's wife."

"That's me. Murdo's out on his rounds. Can I help you?"

"You might be the very person."

"Come in. I was just about to have a cup of coffee."

Hamish followed her into a bright living room. "Sit yourself down," she said, "and I'll bring you a cup. Scones?"

"Yes, please."

She left and came back after a short time carrying a laden tray, which she set on a table by the window. "We'll have our coffee here," she said. "I do so hate crouching over a coffee table."

Once she had served Hamish with scones and coffee, she asked, "What seems to be the problem?"

"It's Geordie McArthur up the brae from the Strathbane

road. I feel he's treating his wife right cruel and all in the name o' religion. He doesn't let her go out. She looks worn down. He's jealous o' the very air she breathes. I tackled him on it, and he said I was an emissary of Satan."

"Does he beat her?"

"I don't think so." The scones were like bricks. He left one half-eaten on his plate. He thought the minister's wife must have been taking baking lessons from Angela Brodie, who was a notoriously bad cook.

"You mean it's mental cruelty?"

"Yes."

"I'll see what I can do. I'll tell Murdo, and he will pay Geordie a visit. Goodness, these scones are quite terrible. I bought them this morning in Patel's. I must be having a word with him. They had a label, 'Local home baking.'"

"I tell you what, pack them up," said Hamish. "I'm going into Lochdubh, and I'll speak to Mr. Patel about them."

"That's very good of you. I'll get a bag."

When she ushered him out, she said, "Don't worry about Mrs. McArthur. We'll sort something out."

Hamish stopped at Patel's and carried the bag into the shop. He dumped it on the counter. "Did Angela Brodie supply you with these scones?"

"Yes, I told the local women I would sell any of their home baking they liked to give me. Mrs. Brodie said baking would be a welcome change from writing."

"They're awful," said Hamish. "I'll buy what you've got left, and then you tell her you've cancelled the scheme."

"But some of the cakes the others bake are very good!"

"Angela can only bake scones and shortbread. Tell her there's no market."

Hamish bought the rest of the scones. He wrapped them tightly and dropped them in a rubbish bin in the front. Then he realised the television vans had gone and there wasn't a reporter in sight.

His insides cringed as he heard himself being hailed by Blair. Blair's piggy eyes were gleaming with malice. "Step inside the unit, laddie. I've something to show you."

Hamish followed him in.

"That's Gannon's desk ower there," said Blair.

On the wall behind the inspector's desk was a large poster of a highlander wearing nothing more than a tam-o'-shanter, a tartan scarf, a cheesy smile, and a large erection.

"I cannae wait to see old thunder thigh's face," chortled Blair, rubbing his fat hands together. "It's high time she learned to put a smile on her face."

And she'll wipe the smile off yours, thought Hamish. I'm not going to warn you what she'll do. Aloud, he said, "I got to go. Reports to write."

In the police station, Hamish fed Sonsie and Lugs and then went into the police office and began to work. At one point, he heard a woman's voice raised in fury. Then all was silent. He wrote long and detailed reports, attached Mrs. Barret-Wilkinson's hotel receipt to the report on her, printed out the reports, and went out of the station to deliver them to the mobile police unit. He stopped in his tracks.

Outside the mobile unit stood Mary Gannon, Blair, and Superintendent Daviot. Daviot was holding the crumpled poster in his hand.

"I don't care if it's a murder investigation," Daviot was saying to Blair. "You are coming back to headquarters with me. You, too, Inspector."

Jimmy Anderson arrived. Daviot ordered him to take charge of the investigation. He drove off with Blair and Mary following in their cars.

Hamish told Jimmy the reason for the ruckus, and Jimmy yelled with delight. "The whisky's on me, Hamish. Blair must ha' gone mad. What if one of the press had called in at the unit, seen that poster, and photographed it? It would have been front page o' the *News of the World*."

"Let's hope he gets suspended," said Hamish. "Here's my reports, Jimmy. I would like to interview that Miss Creedy again. I want to know what guilty secret she has, if any."

Before Hamish drove off to Lochdubh, he took out his mobile phone and called Elspeth and told her about Geordie's Land Rover. He felt he owed her some news in return for her research. "Don't worry about Miss Creedy. I'll tackle her again myself. Call at the police station this evening," said Hamish, "and I'll see if I can let you have anything else. Where have all the press gone?"

"Hostage situation in Perth. Young children involved. Luke's rushed off to cover it, although the Perth man is furious at him invading his patch. See you later."

☼　　☼　　☼

Miss Creedy's shop was closed, and a For Sale sign was in the window. Hamish retreated to the Land Rover and looked up the local phone book. She lived, he noticed, in the same council estate as Mrs. Gillespie.

She was working in her small front garden when he arrived. She started when she saw him, made a move as if to run indoors, and then stood her ground.

"I have talked and talked to the police," she said, her voice shrill with fear. "I have nothing more to say."

"Yes, you have." Hamish took a gamble. "Mrs. Gillespie was blackmailing you, and I know it. I think we should go into the house."

Miss Creedy began to cry, great gulping sobs racking her thin body. Hamish guided her into the house.

When she was seated, he pulled a seat up in front of her and faced her.

"Why did you do it?" he asked when she finally dried her eyes.

"It was the price," she said. "I'd ordered the tourist stuff before from a factory in Strathbane. Then one day, this Chinaman called at the shop and said he had an import-export business in Glasgow. There was a factory in China that made the stuff so cheap, Scottish tourist things, in fact tourist things for a lot of countries, and he could let me have cheap stock. I thought nothing of it. It seemed all right to order from him and save a lot of money.

"I had to answer the phone in the back shop one day and Mrs. Gillespie had dropped in, so I asked her if she would mind the shop. The order book was open on the counter. She must have read it. She said she would tell the local newspaper that all my Scottish tourist goods came from China. The shame! I pleaded with her. She said she wouldn't say anything if I let her win at bingo. It was horribly easy. She gave me a bingo card with numbers on it. I made sure those were the only numbers to be called.

"Now it's all come out, and you're going to arrest me for fraud. I'd rather kill myself. I thought if I could sell the shop, I might get enough to move somewhere far from here."

Hamish thought rapidly. If he took her in, she would be brutally interrogated by Blair, and she would certainly be charged. Even if she did not kill herself, her life would be over. Such as Miss Creedy just couldn't bear the shame.

"Where were you the night Shona Fraser was murdered?"

"I was with my sister in Inverness. I went down for a visit and stayed overnight. I gave that detective her address and phone number."

"Look, I tell you what I'll do," said Hamish. "We'll keep this between us. You overreacted. The locals don't buy tourist things. They really would have thought nothing of it. When you sell your shop, you'll work out just how much money Mrs. Gillespie illegally got at the bingo, then we'll see Father McNulty, and you'll hand the money back."

She leaned forward and clasped his hands. "Oh, thank you! I've been such a fool."

"It's amazing how decent people can be made to feel guilty over little things," said Hamish. "Mrs. Gillespie preyed on that guilt. Have the police asked you about the bingo? I'm afraid I put in my report that Mrs. Gillespie might have been forcing you to cheat."

"Yes, they did. But I lied, and poor Father McNulty, believing me innocent, backed me up."

"Right. We'll let the matter drop. They'll have checked out your alibi, and you probably won't have a visit from them again. So keep quiet until this is all over."

"Thank you. I shall be in your debt for the rest of my life." She looked at him with adoring eyes.

"Enough o' that!" Alarmed, Hamish got to his feet. "Chust forget about it."

"I must repay you. You are a bachelor. I—I could bake you cakes and clean your house and—"

"*No!* Leave me alone. It'll look suspicious to the police if you start hanging around."

He left hurriedly as she followed him to the Land Rover, babbling thanks.

Hamish drove a short distance round the next corner and stopped outside Mr. Gillespie's house.

Mr. Gillespie was at home. He looked frail but happy. "Come in," he said.

The living room was a clutter of books and DVDs.

Hamish removed his cap and sat down. "Your late wife was a blackmailer," he said. "Did she just work for those five people—Professor Sander, Mrs. Fleming, Mrs. Wellington, Mrs. Styles, and Mrs. Barret-Wilkinson?"

"As far as I know. One day a week each. She did say she was thinking of leaving Mrs. Wellington."

"You're not shocked your wife was a blackmailer?"

"No. Man, I'd started to hate her a long while ago. Nothing awful about her would surprise me."

"You used to have a good steady job. Why did she take to cleaning?"

"She liked it. I mean, she'd even clean the place to bits here. It's a sort of power."

"Has anyone come to see you to ask about her effects? Old letters, things like that?"

He shook his head.

"Did your wife have any close friends, even in the past?"

"Not that I can think of."

Hamish gave up and left him. His thoughts turned to the formidable Mrs. Styles. Was she as squeaky-clean as she seemed?

He phoned Jimmy. "Any news on the post-mortem on Mrs. Samson?"

"Aye, the procurator fiscal says it was a heart attack, pure and simple. So that's one murder less. The mobile unit's packing up. They feel they've got everything out your village they can."

"This Mrs. Styles," said Hamish. "What was her alibi?"

"I don't think anyone asked her. She's such a formidable church person that I think the powers-that-be decided to give her a miss."

"I'll try her," said Hamish, "but be prepared for an angry report about police harassment."

*   *   *

Hamish was informed by a neighbour that Mrs. Styles was round at the church. He made his way to the Church of Scotland and pushed open the door. Mrs. Styles was up in the pulpit, polishing the wings of the brass eagle which held the Bible.

Hamish wondered whether to trick her into an admission the way he had tricked Miss Creedy, but decided against it. Such as Mrs. Styles would not be easily frightened.

In the organ loft, the organist began to play Bach's Toccata and Fugue. Dracula music, thought Hamish as Mrs. Styles grasped the brass eagle and glared down at him.

She slowly descended the stairs from the pulpit and approached him, a can of brass polish in one hand and a cleaning rag in the other.

"What is it, Officer?" she demanded.

"I wanted to ask you some more questions about Mrs. Gillespie."

"What?" She swung round and glared up at the organ loft. "Stop that noise," she shouted. "I can't hear myself think."

The organist ceased abruptly. "What I was wondering . . . ," began Hamish.

But the organist burst into a jaunty rendition of "These Boots Are Made for Walking," filling the church with noise.

"Outside," mouthed Mrs. Styles.

They walked out into the graveyard. "That man!" exclaimed Mrs. Styles. "I have complained and complained about him, but no one will listen to me. He's a sacrilegious disgrace, that's what he is. Now, what do you want?"

"Mrs. Gillespie, as has been well established, was a blackmailer. I am not suggesting for a minute that she was blackmailing you . . ."

"You'd better not! I'm a respectable woman."

"Nobody said you weren't. But Mrs. Gillespie had a nasty way of poking and prying through her employers' private papers. Did you ever catch her at it?"

"Yes, I did. But I gave her a sound lecture. She was not a good cleaner, and I was going to fire her."

"Why didn't you?"

"Because I am a Christian. And when she told me she had terminal cancer and that the work was the only thing that kept her mind off her impending death, I kept her on and was lenient with her."

"When did she tell you this?"

"Six months ago. Her work had become really slack."

"Her husband is the one who has cancer. There was nothing up with her. If she'd had cancer, it would have shown in the autopsy."

"I wish I had never let that woman in my house. The more I hear about her, the more horrible she seems."

Hamish studied Mrs. Styles. She was clear-eyed and arrogant. He was perfectly sure she was telling the truth. Perhaps, he thought, if she'd had a guilty secret, she might have been a more likeable woman.

"Mrs. Styles, if you hear of anything, know anything, please let me know. You can phone me at the police station in Lochdubh."

"I am an honest woman, I'll have you know. If I did know of anything, I would have told the police already."

And that was that, thought Hamish gloomily.

He went back and drove off up into the hills. He finally stopped, got out, and walked to the edge of a cliff above the boiling Atlantic. The waves were hypnotic in their driving immensity as they hurled themselves against the base of the cliff. The air was full of spray. Cormorants rose up from the cliffs and then dived headlong into the sea. A puffin emerged from its burrow on the cliff top, regarded Hamish, and dived back into its burrow again.

I'm tired of police work, thought Hamish suddenly. I'm weary of people like Blair and Mary Gannon pushing me around. It wouldn't be any better if I went for promotion. They'd shut down the police station as quickly as anything.

But if, he mused, I resigned, they'd put the police station up for sale. With the reward I got from the bank for stopping that robbery last year, I could put a down payment and get a mortgage. I would become a full-time crofter. Hardly any money in that, but I need very little to live on. I could do odd jobs. The locals don't like working for the newcomers, and there are more of them moving north. I'd be free.

He smiled as he watched the diving gulls and the flying spray.

Hamish decided to head for Lochdubh. He was looking forward to seeing Blair's face when he learned he was leaving the force. A little cloud crept up on the horizon of his mind. Blair would be delighted and Mary Gannon indifferent.

He banished the cloud and walked back to the Land Rover with a spring in his step.

✳   ✳   ✳

Once back in his office, Hamish typed out his resignation and then drove to police headquarters in Strathbane, whistling away.

He decided to hand his resignation in to Superintendent Daviot. Go right to the top, that was the answer.

Helen, the secretary, threw him a look of dislike. "You have not got an appointment," she said. "Mr. Daviot is busy."

The door to the superintendent's office, which had not been quite closed, swung open to reveal Daviot putting golf balls into a paper cup.

"Ah, Hamish," he said, "come in."

Helen leapt to bar the way. "I was just telling this constable that you are busy."

"That's all right, Helen. What is it?"

At that moment, Hamish's mobile phone rang. He drew it out and was about to switch it off when Daviot said good-naturedly, "You can answer that. It might be something to do with the case."

Elspeth's urgent voice came on the line. "You're about to do something stupid, Hamish. Please don't do it until you speak to me."

"How did you . . . ?"

"It doesn't matter. I'm at the hotel. Come and see me."

Hamish rang off.

"Now, Macbeth," said Daviot, "what seems to be the problem?"

Cursing Elspeth in his mind, Hamish crushed the letter in his hand and pinned a pious look on his face. "I chust wondered if Mr. Blair was all right. I heard a rumour he was ill."

Daviot's face darkened. "That is good of you, but at the moment, Detective Chief Inspector Blair is suspended from duty."

"Why?"

"I appreciate your concern, but it is nothing to do with you, so go about your duties."

Hamish reflected angrily on Elspeth's psychic powers, which he only half believed in. He screeched to a halt in front of the hotel and marched in.

Elspeth was waiting for him at the reception desk, her face anxious. "Come into the bar," said Hamish, "and tell me what the hell you were talking about."

When they were seated at a corner table, Elspeth said nervously, "It's like this. I'd a sudden awful feeling you were about to leave in the middle of this case. You were fed up and worried and then you felt free."

"I wass about to hand in my resignation," said Hamish bleakly, the strengthening of his accent revealing he was upset. "I am that fed up wi' being pushed here and ordered there by the likes o' Blair and Gannon. And dinnae tell me it's a' my ain fault for not moving up the ranks. I'm frustrated by lack o' information at every turn."

"I would only point out that a mere copper isn't given all the information, but I won't."

"Not Irish, are you?" asked Hamish sarcastically.

"Hamish, you've got to press on. You can't walk away from this. Just think how you would feel if you did and the murders were never solved. Think of the black suspicion in Braikie.

They would start to think the husband had done it. They'd make his life a misery. And what of poor Shona? Her parents came here from Glasgow yesterday. They're devastated. They need a resolution. Let's go down to the police station and make notes. I'll be your Watson. Let's go over everyone from the beginning."

In the police station, Hamish made coffee, and they both went through to the police office.

"Right," said Elspeth. "The first. Professor Sander."

"There's a good chance he pinched one of his students' book on Byron," said Hamish. "But the student is dead. The prof has no real alibi, and he was the nearest person to Mrs. Gillespie. From the post-mortem, it seems she had only been dead for a short time before I found her. So he could have followed her down the drive and struck her in a fit of rage."

"I'll dig a bit more into his background for you. Next?"

"Mrs. Fiona Fleming. Mrs. Samson seemed to think that Mrs. Gillespie believed her to have killed her husband by pushing him down the stairs. I've a feeling in my bones that the man's death was an accident, pure and simple. Maybe Mrs. Fleming was in the early stages of her affair with Dr. Renfrew, and Mrs. Gillespie was blackmailing her over that. I don't like the woman, and I feel she could be quite vicious. But no. I think it was someone cold, calculating, and ruthless. Maybe someone who met Mrs. Gillespie at the foot of the drive and said, 'Let me help you put your stuff in your car,' and then swung the bucket hard."

"Now comes Mrs. Styles."

"The saint of Braikie. I don't think so. I think if Mrs. Gillespie had tried to blackmail her, she would have gone straight to the police. The same with Mrs. Wellington."

"Mrs. Barret-Wilkinson?"

"I can't get the hang o' that woman. She's playing at being the country lady. But she's got a good alibi for the time of Shona's death."

"What alibi?"

"On the night of Shona's murder, she was staying with a friend in Glasgow. Then she had a hotel receipt from the Palace in Inverness. Says she stopped there on the road back."

"What about Dr. Renfrew?"

"He must have been terrified that she'd gossip about his malpractice suit. Could be. Then there's Miss Creedy, who admits to having rigged the bingo so that Mrs. Gillespie would win. I want that kept quiet. I don't believe for a moment she murdered anyone."

"What about Mrs. Gillespie's stepdaughter?"

"Damn! I'd completely forgotten about the lassie. I suppose she'll have been asked for an alibi for the time Shona was murdered, but I'd better have a talk with her again."

"Let's go back to Mrs. Barret-Wilkinson," said Elspeth. "I wonder if a friend would lie for her?"

"Strathclyde police will have checked out her alibi."

"It's not their case. It would be interesting to get down there and suss out whether she might be lying."

"I can't take the time off to go down there. They'd be down on me like a ton o' bricks."

Elspeth looked at him mischievously. "And you don't want to lose your job?"

Hamish gave her a reluctant smile. "You're right. That was a real daft moment I had. Thanks. You scare me sometimes, Elspeth. Do you always know what people are thinking?"

"No, hardly ever, and when I'm down in the city, not at all. Put it down to a lucky guess. Tell you what, if you see the daughter, I'll nip back to Glasgow and interview Mrs. Barret-Wilkinson's alibi. What's her name and address?"

Hamish consulted his notes. "Bella Robinson, The Croft, Mylie Road, Bearsden."

"I'll have a go."

They both stood up. Hamish looked down at Elspeth. He had a sudden longing to take her in his arms. As if she sensed his feelings, Elspeth gave an awkward little duck of her head and muttered, "Goodbye. Talk to you later."

Elspeth wondered whether to tell Luke where she was going, but finally decided against it. Luke had said he didn't come north to work. He was on holiday, and Elspeth's wanting to be a reporter night and day was interfering with good drinking time. And Luke drank a lot. Reporters were hard-drinking people, but Elspeth felt uneasily that Luke's drinking was getting out of hand. Usually the most boozed-up reporter would chase any story, whether on holiday or not.

As she drove south over the Grampian mountains, she put Luke from her mind and, with an even greater effort, stopped thinking about one village policeman.

When she finally got to the respectable town of Bearsden

and found that The Croft was in fact a neat bungalow, she was tired and hungry and wished she had stopped for food on the road.

Her heart sank as she walked up the garden path. Houses with nobody at home always, to Elspeth, radiated an empty feeling. She had debated telephoning first but knew that if by any remote chance Bella had been covering for her friend, she would be forewarned. She rang the bell and waited and waited.

Depressed, she turned away. She went to the bungalow next door and rang the bell.

The woman who answered the door was a large matron with a well-upholstered bosom and thick flowing hair. She looked like the figurehead on an old sailing ship.

"Ye-es?" she asked.

"I was looking for Mrs. Robinson next door," said Elspeth.

"Mrs. Robinson hes goan to hir wee house in Spain." She had the strangled, genteel accents of what is damned as Kelvinside.

"When did she leave?"

"Thet would be yesterday."

Nothing more to do, thought Elspeth wearily. She drove to her Glasgow flat, planning to spend the night before starting on the long journey north. She phoned Hamish. His mobile was switched off. She tried the police station and got his answering service and left a message.

*   *   *

Hamish was in the local pub on the harbour, trying to comfort Archie Maclean. A crumpled letter lay on the scarred table between them.

"Buggering government," said Archie, tears running down his face. "To decommission my boat! To order me to take her to Denmark where she is to be scrapped! The *Sally Jane*'s my life. I'll die without her. What am I goin' tae do?"

"Leave it to me," said Hamish. "I'll get up a petition."

Archie scrubbed his eyes with his sleeve. "Good o' ye, Hamish, but that's been tried afore."

The British government had massacred more than half the Scottish fishing fleet to prevent the waters being overfished.

"Are they offering compensation?"

"Only a wee bit. I didn't go in for the voluntary decommissioning."

"I'll see what I can do."

Hamish went out and along to the church, which was never locked. He seized the bell rope and began to ring the bell. It clamoured out over the village of Lochdubh, bringing people hurrying out of their houses and the minister and his wife from the manse. They knew it was only rung in times of peril. The old folk said it had been rung during World War II when a fishing boat sighted a German destroyer.

"What is going on?" panted Mrs. Wellington.

The villagers began to stream in as Hamish went up to the pulpit. "The government has ordered Archie Maclean's boat to be decommissioned. He's to take her to a scrapyard in Denmark. I want someone to start a petition."

"I'll do that," shouted Mrs. Wellington.

"That'll be a start," said Hamish. "But we'll need more than that. I'll see if there are any press left up at the hotel and try to get them interested."

Mr. Patel ran to his shop and came back with reams of typing paper. A table was set up, and people crowded around to sign.

Hamish came down from the pulpit and, after adding his name to the list, headed up to the Tommel Castle Hotel. "Are any of the national press still here?" he asked Mr. Johnson.

"The television people have gone, but there's two nationals, a French newspaper, and some of the Scottish ones. You'll find them in the bar."

Hamish walked into the bar, a sudden bold idea striking him.

Luke was there, his eyes blurred with drink.

"Gentlemen of the press!" shouted Hamish. "I have a story that will interest you."

Silence fell.

"Archie Maclean, a local fisherman, is having his boat forcibly decommissioned, and he has been ordered to take her to a scrapyard in Denmark."

Bored eyes stared at him. Just another poor fisherman out of work. They'd heard it all before.

"And so," said Hamish, raising his voice, "the villagers are that mad wi' the government that they are declaring independence for Lochdubh."

Now he had their attention. Several were already wondering if a headline "The Mouse That Roared" might be too old hat.

"If you will follow me down to the church hall, you'll see what I mean."

Hamish sprinted out and drove fast back to the hall, where the whole village was now crowded around the petition table.

"I've declared Lochdubh independent," he shouted. "The press are coming. Stick to the story."

A big forester asked, "Can we put up roadblocks into the village and ask them for their passports?"

"Great idea," said Hamish. "But quick. I can hear them coming. Some of you drag me along to the police station and lock me in the cell."

The press arrived just in time to see Hamish being frog-marched along the waterfront. Thank goodness for all those mobile phones with cameras in them, thought Hamish. This'll be on television tomorrow.

He was locked in the one cell in the police station with his dog and cat. They handed the key through the bars to him "chust in case you feel hungry during the night," and headed off.

Hamish then phoned Elspeth and told her the story. "Oh, Hamish, I'm so tired, but I can't miss out on a story like this. I'll drive through the night."

Although not much visited by tourists, Lochdubh was a very scenic highland village. By next morning, the story was round the world. Film of a crumpled and sobbing Archie Maclean was beamed into homes from the north of Scotland to Japan.

Police contingents, roaring over from Strathbane, found

their way barred by roadblocks manned by locals with deer hunting rifles and shotguns.

Blair tried to land in the police helicopter but was driven off by rockets fired up at him—not army rockets, but ones left over from the last fireworks display.

Some wag had found a skull and crossbones used in an amateur production of *The Pirates of Penzance* and had run it up the flagpole on the waterfront. Only the press were allowed past the barriers.

Hamish was photographed in his cell. "This is an outrage," he was quoted as saying, "but on the other hand, I can't say I blame them."

He hoped desperately that the London reaction he was counting on could have its effect before the police decided to use force.

In Number 10 Downing Street, the prime minister, Simon Turl, paced up and down. His popularity had been fading fast. He was addicted to photo opportunities and grabbing headlines and therefore shoved through unpopular acts of Parliament without even considering the consequences.

"How am I to handle this?" he asked his adviser, Sandy McGowan.

"Oh, stop dithering, man. It's simple," growled Sandy. "Say that wee fisherman got the wrong papers by mistake and there's to be an enquiry. Do it fast. Take the wind out of those villagers' sails. No prosecutions."

"But other fishermen will try the same trick."

"It won't be newsworthy if they do. Copycat stories never are. Get on with it."

"Perhaps I should fly up there myself. I can see myself standing on the habour . . ."

"And getting stoned by the locals. I'll handle it. You're due at the House."

Superintendent Daviot gave orders for police to be fitted out in riot gear and armed with stun guns and tear gas.

They arrived in force at the barricade on the Strathbane road.

The villagers on guard raised their guns, their faces grim.

Daviot opened his mouth to give the order to charge when his phone rang. It was his secretary, Helen. "The prime minister's office phoned. You're to stand down. The papers sent to Archie Maclean were a mistake. No one is to be charged with anything. It's to be calmed down and out of the newspapers as quickly as possible."

The villagers manning the barricade watched uneasily. Then Daviot approached the barrier.

"The decommissioning papers were sent to Mr. Maclean by mistake. So take down this ridiculous roadblock. I would arrest the lot of you, but I have orders from Number 10 that there are to be no prosecutions."

Hamish, in his cell, heard the cheering. He unlocked his cell and walked outside the police station.

Villagers were surging along to meet the cheering men returning from the roadblock.

Archie Maclean saw Hamish and cried, "There he is! There's my hero!"

The crowd gathered around Hamish and lifted him up and carried him in triumphal procession from one end of the waterfront to the other.

Up on the Strathbane road on a crest of the hill looking down on the village stood Inspector Mary Gannon.

"Give me a pair of binoculars, someone," she shouted.

A policeman handed her a pair. She lifted them to her eyes, focussed them, and glared down at the magnified sight of Hamish Macbeth being carried round the village.

"So that rogue policeman is responsible for this fiasco," she muttered. "What a waste of police time. I'll have that man."

She turned to the woman police sergeant beside her. "Keep your handcuffs ready," she said, "and follow me."

The triumphal procession carrying Hamish was heading for the pub when they found themselves confronted by one very angry police inspector.

"Put him down!" shouted Mary. "Hamish Macbeth, I am arresting you for inciting riot. Anything you—"

"No, no," said Archie, glaring up at her. "This is by way of an apology. We locked the poor man up in his cell. He had nothing to do with it at all."

Mary faced the crowd. "Is this the truth?"

There came a chorus of agreement.

Mary suddenly knew she had made a terrible mistake. She saw she was being filmed and recorded for television. She knew Number 10 wanted the story killed. She did not believe for a moment that Archie had been sent the wrong papers. She would be blamed for keeping the story running.

Mary turned on her heel and marched away.

Hamish fled to his police station and locked himself in to keep away from the press.

Then a note was shoved through the letter box. It read, "Let me in. Elspeth."

Chapter Nine

My barmie noddle's working prime.

—Robert Burns

Hamish opened the door. "Come in, quick," he said.

Elspeth slid in. She looked tired. "Great story, Hamish. I've been filing stories since I got back from Glasgow, and I haven't had any sleep."

"I think I'll have a whisky," said Hamish. "Feel like joining me? I felt at one moment I'd made an awful mistake. I could see the poor Currie sisters with their eyes streaming with tear gas and some of the locals being shot with stun guns."

"I'm surprised our divine leader didn't fly up. He and his wife breathe photo opportunities."

"Maybe he was frightened he'd be massacred. Whisky?"

"Yes, I'll join you, and then I'm going to bed."

"Alone?"

"What sort of question is that?" demanded Elspeth angrily. "And what right have you to ask it?"

"I'm sorry," said Hamish. "I don't know why I asked that. Stop bristling at me and sit down. You look like Sonsie when the cat's fur is up."

"Where are the beasts?"

"Out for a walk. I lifted them out through the kitchen window."

"How will you know when they want back in?"

"Sonsie leaps up and raps on the glass."

"What came over that police inspector? Daviot said there were to be no arrests. Made a good story, though."

"You didn't, did you?"

"We all did. Why did she do it? She struck me as a career police officer."

"I think she likes the authority her position gives her. I think someone like me really annoys her. Where's Luke?"

"Up at the hotel with the other press. Mr. Johnson will be glad when the story dies down because he can't give any tourists a booking. The press have taken up most of the rooms."

"Isn't that good for business?"

"Not really. The hotel relies on regulars to come back year after year. Most of the press will be gone by tomorrow."

Hamish poured two shots of whisky and put a jug of water on the table.

"Aren't you going to open your mail?" asked Elspeth, looking at a few unopened letters on the kitchen table.

"Probably bills. I'll look at them tomorrow."

Elspeth flipped through them. "Here's one that looks personal, and the postmark's Inverness."

"Let me see." Hamish opened the envelope and scanned the letter inside.

"Well, I'll be damned," he said.

"Probably," said Elspeth. "What is it?"

"It's from Mr. Abercrombie, that student's father, you know the one who claimed that Sander had stolen his book. He says a woman came to visit him the other day and said she was a friend of his son's and that they'd been at university at the same time. She was shocked to learn Sean was dead. She said she remembered Professor Sander had given him a job typing out his manuscript, a book on Byron. She said Sean went a bit mad after that and started claiming the book was his own. He kept swearing to come off the drugs."

"So that's one blackmailing theory out the window," said Elspeth.

"No, on the contrary. There must be something else. Someone as pompous as the professor wouldn't put up with a bossy charwoman unless she had something on him. Inspector Gannon wanted me to follow him. Maybe she was on to something. I think I'll get back on it tomorrow. I'll have a talk to the stepdaughter first. She may have remembered something."

"I'll come with you," volunteered Elspeth.

"You'll get me in trouble. I'm not supposed to have civilians in a police vehicle unless I'm arresting them."

"But, idiot, we'll take my car. You don't want to be seen tailing him in a cop car."

"Forgot that. I took Angela's car the last time. But the neighbours saw me parked out all day and called the police."

"A couple is better camouflage. Let's guess it's something

to do with where he goes outside Braikie. In order to go to Strathbane or Inverness, he'd need to go along the main street. So we wait there."

Hamish still hesitated. Elspeth surveyed him with amusement. "Yes, Hamish, we will take your odd animals so you don't need to sit there working up courage to ask Angela to look after them for you."

"Thanks. Angela was getting fed up with me. I'll meet you here about noon. That'll give me time to go and see the stepdaughter."

The following day was fine, with only an edge of cold heralding the coming of the long, dark Scottish winter. The very mountains in the distance were blue, as if taking their colour from the cloudless sky above.

The sea opposite Heather Gillespie's house was calm. Seals lay on the beach, basking in the sunlight. At the sound of Hamish's approaching vehicle, they started to waddle towards the sea like so many arthritic and elderly gentlemen.

To Hamish's surprise, Tom Morrison, Heather's exhusband, answered the door. "Surprised to see me?" he said with a grin. "We're back together. We'll be getting married again next month."

"That's grand," said Hamish. "Is Heather at home?"

"Come in. I'll get her."

When Heather appeared, she looked happy. Hamish hoped it would not turn out that she had murdered her mother in a fit of rage. He suddenly wondered why it was when he had been stalking the professor that the neighbours had all noticed his presence and yet had seen no one at all on the day of Mrs. Gillespie's murder. Could someone have masqueraded as a postman, or as someone the neighbours would expect to see?

He realised Heather was looking at him with amusement. "I've asked you two times if you want tea or coffee," she said.

"Sorry, I suddenly thought of something. Nothing for me, thanks. I wondered if you had remembered anything about your stepmother that might be useful."

"I don't think I can. Apart from humiliating me and breaking up my marriage, I don't really know what else she got up to."

"Did she ever hint that she had some sort of power over any of her employers?"

"No, she was too busy exercising power over me and Dad. I'm glad she's dead. Dad's cancer has gone into remission. They say it's a miracle."

"I know you've had a lot on your mind, what with the murder of your mother and getting your marriage back together, but when you get a quiet moment, think of anything she might have found out about anyone and let slip."

She promised and Hamish left. Now to meet Elspeth and follow the professor.

It was a long and boring day for Hamish and Elspeth. As evening approached, Hamish began to feel irritable because of the attraction Elspeth held for him. He wanted to say something and yet feared a rejection. Also, he knew Elspeth would settle for nothing less than marriage, and he really didn't feel he wanted to get married.

Suddenly Elspeth said, "There he goes!" They set off in pursuit of the professor.

Elspeth was driving. "Keep well back," Hamish warned her. "The roads are so empty, and we don't want him catching sight of us."

Professor Sander took the Strathbane road, and Hamish groaned. "Maybe that bookshop he visited last time is open late. He'll buy books and head back home. A whole day wasted."

"May as well keep going," said Elspeth, negotiating a hair-pin bend. "I'll be glad when we get to the straight bit. That way I can keep him in sight from a long way off."

As soon as she saw the professor's car disappear into the town, she accelerated.

"I've lost him," she mourned.

"No, you haven't," said Hamish. "I just saw him turning into the multi-storey car park."

There were two cars now behind the professor looking for parking spaces. Professor Sander parked on the third floor. Elspeth slid her car into a bay a little way away.

When the professor got out and walked to the lift, they both headed for the stairs and sprinted down.

The streets were busy, so they were able to follow him easily without being seen.

Then, to their surprise, their quarry turned into a McDonald's.

"We can't go in there," said Elspeth. "He'd see us."

"Let's wait across the road. He surely won't be long. It's fast food."

After only twenty minutes, Sander emerged and headed for the car park.

"The wee scunner is going home," complained Hamish.

"You never know," said Elspeth. "Let's get the car and follow."

But the professor's car veered off on a road down to the docks. They followed, hanging well back.

"Stop here," said Hamish. "He can't go much further. This road's a dead end. Let's get out and have a look."

Keeping in the shadow of dark warehouses, still smelling of soot, they crept forward. The professor's car had stopped, but the engine was still running.

Three youths emerged from the shadows. "I hope he isn't going to be mugged," muttered Elspeth. "Then we'd have to do something."

They saw Professor Sander lower the car window. "Is it drugs?" whispered Elspeth. "Seems to be some sort of deal going on."

Then two of the youths melted back into the shadows, and one went round to the passenger side of the car and got in.

"Not drugs," said Hamish. "Rent boy. In the front of the car so a quick blow job. Should be over soon."

"Are you going to arrest them?"

"I got a good look at the boy from the light in the car when he leaned over with the others. He's over age."

"But still . . ."

"It goes on the whole time in this dump of a town," said Hamish wearily. "Prostitutes, rent boys, drugs, the lot. But now I can call on him tomorrow and find out if this is the reason Mrs. Gillespie may have been blackmailing him. I am not going to single the professor out and ruin his life. Can you imagine what Blair would make of this?"

"I heard Blair had been suspended."

"Probably back on the job. The way that man oils up to his superiors is little short of genius. Let's go."

They walked back to Elspeth's car and got in.

"I'm beginning to think Braikie is a den of iniquity," said Elspeth.

"I'm sure none of us would like our private lives dug into," said Hamish.

"Can I come with you to the professor's tomorrow?"

"Now, Elspeth, how do I explain bringing the press along? And remember, all this is off the record. Stop the car when we're clear of the town. I need to feed the beasts, and I'm right hungry myself."

Back home, Hamish checked his answering machine and was surprised to find there were no messages for him at all. He had been sure that either Blair or Mary Gannon would have been on the phone, demanding to know what he was doing.

He washed and undressed and got into bed, followed by the dog and cat. "You'd better stay here yourselves tomorrow," he told them. He suddenly found himself wishing that Elspeth, instead of his animals, were lying beside him. But Elspeth was no longer interested in an affair. It would need to be marriage.

✳   ✳   ✳

Hamish was prepared to handle the matter of the rent boy delicately—and wished for years afterwards that he had done so—but Professor Sander greeted him with an initial tirade about police harassment and the stupidity of local coppers which he put down to inbreeding.

So Hamish came right out with it. "What were you doing soliciting a rent boy in Strathbane last night?"

Hamish had been kept on the doorstep. The professor's face turned a muddy colour. "Come in," he said faintly.

Hamish followed him into his study. Professor Sander sank down into a chair and stared at the floor.

"Is that what Mrs. Gillespie had on you?" Hamish demanded.

"I invited one of them back here." The bluster had left the professor, and Hamish had to strain to hear what he was saying. "We got drunk and he stayed the night. When I came down in the morning, I found him in the kitchen with Mrs. Gillespie. It was after that the blackmailing started."

"What did she ask for?"

"Money, of course. But also, she treated me like a servant. If she wanted to go to Inverness, say, I had to drive her. One time, I had to buy her an expensive new television and DVD player. I couldn't go to the police."

"Did you kill her?"

"No, I did not. When I saw her dead, all I felt was relief." Then some of his old bluster came back. "You must have been following me," he said. "That's harassment. You bring me down, and I'll have you out of a job. I have powerful friends."

So instead of reassuring him that he would keep the matter

quiet, Hamish said, "You'll need your powerful friends. You'll be hearing from me again."

He drove to the Tommel Castle Hotel, where Elspeth had told him she would be waiting to hear how he had got on.

She listened carefully and then turned those odd silver eyes of hers on him. "Did you not tell him you wouldn't be reporting him?"

"I was going to, Elspeth, but he began to get all pompous again, and I wanted him to sweat a little. What is this? You were all for me reporting him."

"I've got a bad feeling," said Elspeth. "I know he's a pompous prick, but look at it this way. All that investigation into his book must have put him under a lot of strain. He's probably been behaving himself for quite a bit. Then when he thinks he's safe, he heads off to Strathbane to—er—celebrate. He's probably now thinking of headlines in the papers."

"A man picking up a rent boy doesn't make a story these days."

"But frightened people always think they'll be top of the news. Hamish, I'm begging you. Go and tell the man you're going to keep it quiet."

"Elspeth, when I left him, he seemed quite recovered. Oh, okay, I'll go back and put his mind at rest."

She followed him out to the car park. "You may be too late. Look at the sky!"

Black clouds like long fingers were trailing in from the Atlantic.

"It chust means the rain's coming," said Hamish angrily.

He drove off slowly, aware of Elspeth watching him go.

Rubbish, he thought. He realised he hadn't had any breakfast, so instead he went to the police station and fried sausage, bacon, and eggs and ate leisurely. Then he fed the dog and cat and let them out for a walk before driving off reluctantly in the direction of Braikie. The wind was strengthening, and the sky above was black.

There was a flash of lightning followed by a tremendous crack of thunder. Damn Elspeth and her fancies, he thought. The rain came down, whipping across the landscape.

He was glad the tide was out as he reached the shore road, but out in the Atlantic, huge waves lit by flashes of lightning were rearing up. It seemed like the end of the world, as though the sea were coming back to claim its own, to claim all the glens it had flooded of old. There was something about Sutherland on a bad day, thought Hamish, that made the human race feel like temporary inhabitants of an increasingly angry planet.

He got out of the Land Rover in front of the professor's house and ran up the short drive. He had forgotten to wear his oilskin, and his regulation sweater and trousers were soaked by the time he reached the shelter of the porch.

He rang the bell. No answer. The professor's car was in the drive. He tried the door handle. The door was not locked.

Probably drinking himself silly, thought Hamish. "Professor Sander!" he shouted.

The thunder rolled, but further away.

Hamish went into the study. Maybe gone to bed. He went upstairs, located the professor's bedroom, but it, too, was empty.

Hamish began to feel more cheerful. Elspeth and her thoughts! The man had probably decided to walk to the shops and had got caught in the rain.

But why didn't he lock the door? asked a little voice in his head.

He shrugged and decided to make a thorough search so that he could report to Elspeth that all was well. The sitting room was empty.

He opened the kitchen door, looked in, and then froze.

From a meat hook in the ceiling hung the lifeless body of Professor Sander.

What have I done? thought Hamish. He took out his phone and called police headquarters.

There was a sealed envelope on the kitchen table addressed to the procurator fiscal. He longed to open it. What did it say? Did it say it's because of Hamish Macbeth that I can't live any longer?

He retreated to the hall and sat down on a hard chair by the door and waited.

Blair arrived, followed by Jimmy Anderson, two policemen, and the pathologist. It would have to be Blair, thought Hamish.

"In the kitchen," said Hamish bleakly.

"Stay where you are," growled Blair.

So Hamish stayed. The forensic team arrived.

"So," said Blair, confronting Hamish, "what were you doing here?"

Hamish thought quickly. "It was believed that Professor Sander had plagiarised his book on Byron. Some student had been accusing him of pinching his work. I had just received proof that this was not true and called to tell the professor. I found him dead."

"Get to your feet when you're talking to a senior officer. Well, it wraps those murders up."

"How?" asked Hamish.

"Oh, get back to yer sheep, laddie, and leave things to the experts."

Behind Blair's fat back, Jimmy held up a piece of paper saying, "See you later."

Back at the police station, Hamish phoned Elspeth and told her the news. "I'd better get a police statement, Hamish. I'll get over to Braikie right now. Luke had better come with me."

Luke, thought Hamish after he had rung off. I'd forgotten all about him. He experienced a sudden sharp pang of jealousy.

He did his various crofting chores during the rest of the day. The storm had rolled away to the east, and the day was bright and chilly.

As the first evening star twinkled in the sky, he found his thoughts turning to Elspeth. But a nasty little cautioning voice in his brain asked him whether he would be so interested if she had not arrived with Luke. He tried not to pay any attention to it. He could just see Elspeth living at the police station. It could be fun. He would have company during the long, dark winter months. She would not like to be idle, but she could surely get her old job on the local paper back again.

Then it would be rather grand to have a son. Would she want a big wedding? If she didn't, his mother would.

His happy thoughts were interrupted by the arrival of Jimmy. "Well, that's that," said Jimmy. "Are you going to stand out here looking at your hens with a silly smile on your face all night, or can we go inside?"

Hamish led the way into the kitchen and took down a bottle of whisky and glasses from the cupboard.

"What's what?" he asked.

"That letter Sander left. He said . . . wait a bit. I've taken a note of it." He fished out a battered notebook and thumbed through the leaves. "Ah, here it is. 'I am sorry for everything. Yes, I am guilty. I cannot bear to live with the shame. I would not survive in prison.' It's signed with his name. So that's that. We're still trying to figure out why he killed Mrs. Gillespie except that the blackmailing old trout must have had something on him that Shona found out. Daviot's thrilled to bits. Gave a press conference. All the press are going away. You'll be glad of that."

Hamish slowly poured two measures of whisky. "He didn't do those murders, Jimmy."

"Man, he as good as said so!"

Hamish told Jimmy about the rent boy and about how Mrs. Gillespie had been blackmailing him. "I should have told the professor I wasnae going to do anything about it. But he was so pompous that I decided to let him sweat for a little. God, I've as good as killed him."

"Nasty wee man. No great loss," said Jimmy heartlessly.

"This whisky is foul, Hamish. What's it called? Dream o' the Glens. Probably made in Japan."

"It wass on special offer. If you don't like it, don't drink it. Don't you see the problem? If I tell Blair what I know, he may get me suspended or even fired. They'll all be that furious that their precious case isnae wrapped up."

"Hamish, I can't really sit on this information. I mean, you don't want a murderer getting off scot-free."

"Could you give me a couple of days?"

"Hamish, this isn't the telly where the senior officer says, 'You have twenty-four hours.' And it'll be worse for you if it looks as if you've been sitting on this information. Look, I tell you what I'll do. I'll try to get hold of the rent boy who spent the night with the prof and got caught by Mrs. Gillespie. I'll put in a report about that and suggest it might be the real reason for his suicide. I'll hint that the rent boy was about to blow the gaff. They'll hate me for it."

"Thanks, Jimmy. There iss something nagging at the back of my mind."

"He could have done it, Hamish."

"Let me think about it. I wass surprised not to see Inspector Gannon at the scene."

"She's been transferred to Inverness. Blair, who, as you must have gathered, did not stay suspended long, was heard saying that they wanted none of that feminist crap in Strathbane. Daviot was furious with her for causing what he called 'an unnecessary ruckus.' Sad day for women's lib. The few women police who hoped to rise in the ranks are furious as well, thinking that she's ruined their chances of promotion."

*   *   *

That night, Hamish lay in bed but could not sleep. All the people he had interviewed kept swirling around in his head. Then he suddenly sat bolt upright. Mrs. Gillespie had recognised Dr. Renfrew from a television show. A blackmailer would immediately slot in a video or DVD to record the rest of it. Probably a video. But she had a DVD player. The professor said she had made him buy her one. Maybe it was before that. He phoned the stepdaughter, Heather. Tom Morrison's sleepy voice came on the line. "What do you want?" he asked sharply. "It's two in the morning."

"It's urgent," said Hamish. "I need to speak to Heather."

He could hear a lot of grumbling, and then Heather's voice came on the line.

"Did Mrs. Gillespie tape a lot of television shows?"

"You got me up in the middle of the night to ask that!"

"It's important. Think!"

"Well, yes, but only a few. In fact I was going over to my dad's today to throw out a lot of old stuff. There's a box of videos in the attic."

"What about DVDs?"

"Not them. She couldn't get the hang of how to record them."

"I'll meet you at your father's at seven in the morning."

"Have a heart!"

"Well, make it eight."

Hamish rang off. She liked the Trant Television's reality shows. Maybe, just maybe, she had taped another show because there was someone she recognised. But wouldn't that be too much of a coincidence? On the other hand, often in the past people had moved to the far north of Scotland to escape from something. How long, for example, had Fiona Fleming been living in Braikie? And the impeccable Mrs. Styles had been a gorgeous-looking girl in her youth from what he remembered of the photograph he had seen.

He barely slept that night. He was up early to shave and dress and feed the cat and dog. It was only after he had fed them that he realised his guilty conscience was making them fat because he was giving them too many meals.

Once more he took the road to Braikie under the chill light of a small yellow sun, rising above the mountains.

He was too early when he arrived outside Mr. Gillespie's home. He sat in the Land Rover and fretted until, at last, Heather arrived.

She let him in and said, "Come upstairs, but quiet, now. Dad'll still be asleep. I put a lot of stuff in the spare room. It used to be mine."

She pushed open a door and said, "I'll leave you to it. I've got to have a cup of coffee. You're just in time. The Salvation Army is sending someone round this afternoon to pick the lot up."

Hamish ignored the plastic bags of clothes. "Where are the videos?"

"You'll find them in that box over by the window."

Hamish knelt down on the floor beside the box and began to go through them. There were various films, but six tapes were not marked at all. He'd need to go through the lot.

He carried them down to the kitchen. "Have you a video recorder here?"

"I haven't seen one. I seem to mind she threw it out when she got the DVD player."

Hamish wrote her a receipt for the tapes. He did not have any sort of recorder at the police station. Then he remembered that Angela Brodie had a video recorder.

Angela was cooking breakfast when Hamish arrived. She was placing a plate of sausage, eggs, bacon, fried bread, and black pudding in front of the doctor.

"That'll fur your arteries," commented Hamish.

"Did you interrupt my breakfast to lecture me on diet?" asked Dr. Brodie, taking a swipe at a cat that was trying to drag a sausage off the plate.

Hamish explained that he needed a video recorder.

"There's one in the living room," said Angela. "Help yourself. It's all over the news this morning, Hamish, that the professor committed those murders."

"Maybe," said Hamish.

He went into the living room, switched on the television, and slotted the first of the tapes into the video recorder. It turned out to be the one featuring Dr. Renfrew, amongst others. The next one, also Trant Television, was about shady car dealers. He watched it until the end in case Tom Morrison should appear, but there was nothing there. He took it out and changed it for another. It was an exposé of the number of pirated goods in street markets. His heart sinking, he tried another. It was about antique dealers who faked antiques.

Angela brought him in a cup of coffee. He thanked her, wincing a little as he saw a cat hair sticking to the edge of the cup.

"Got anything?" she asked.

"Nothing," said Hamish.

"You looking for proof of something?"

"I was hoping to find some."

"I'll leave you to it."

Hamish slotted in the fifth tape. He found himself looking at a programme about prostitution. He sighed impatiently as he listened to interviews with prostitutes. He was about to switch off the tape when the presenter said, "Of course, there are still top-flight models, as they are called, on sale at discreet clubs in London. We could not gain access, but we found a film which had been secretly taken at a club in Beauchamp Place in the early nineties." Hamish watched the grainy film. Very beautiful girls were drinking with various men. Must cost a mint for one of those, thought Hamish. And then he saw a familiar figure come into view. Mrs. Barret-Wilkinson! One of the men went up to her and bent down and whispered. She nodded and called one of the girls over. Hamish watched, transfixed, but the brief film ended.

So that was what Mrs. Gillespie had on Mrs. Barret-Wilkinson, he thought, and Shona probably remembered that film.

What about her Glasgow alibi?

He decided to go straight down to Glasgow and see if Bella Robinson had returned.

On the way out, he pleaded with Angela to look after his

animals just one more time and then, deaf to her complaints, hurried to the Land Rover.

He drove straight to Inverness airport and caught a plane to Glasgow. He hired a car at Glasgow airport and set out in the direction of Bearsden, getting lost a few times in Glasgow's bewildering flyovers until he found the right route.

As he braked to a stop outside The Croft, he saw a car parked in the space in front of the house. He went up and rang the bell.

A small woman with dyed-brown hair and a heavily made-up face answered the door.

She looked alarmed when she saw Hamish.

"May I come in?" asked Hamish.

"All right. What's it about?"

Hamish followed her into a living room furnished with a three-piece suite in white leather. A small crystal chandelier hung from the low ceiling, and a gas fire of fake coals hissed in the grate.

He turned to face her. "Why did you lie about Mrs. Barret-Wilkinson staying with you?"

"I didn't know it was a police matter." She had a voice which sounded as if it had been roughened over the years by whisky and cigarettes. "Crystal told me she was having an affair with a married man and his wife was getting suspicious. She said if the wife accused her of anything, she would say she had been staying with me, because she was going to spend the night with him at a hotel in Inverness."

"Didn't it strike you as odd when you heard about the murder of that television researcher?"

She twisted her heavily beringed hands and looked at the floor.

"You're younger than she is," said Hamish. "Were you one of her girls at that club in Beauchamp Place? Don't lie to me. I can find out."

"Yes, I was, and yes, I was frightened when I heard about the murder, so after the police had interviewed me, I cleared off."

"Is her name really Barret-Wilkinson?"

"Yes, she married one of the punters. Did well for herself. Got a mint out of the divorce. I'd got out of the game with enough money to live comfortably. I wasn't like the other girls. No drugs for me."

"Did you think Mrs. Barret-Wilkinson might have killed Shona Fraser?"

"Yes."

"Why?"

She sighed. "Sit down, won't you?"

Hamish took off his cap and sat down. Mrs. Fleming would love this white furniture, he thought.

"It was in '93," she said. "One of the punters wanted her. Crystal used to be on the game but was glad to get the post as a madam. She refused, but the owner, Freddie Ionedes, was in the club that night, and he ordered her to get on with it. I don't know what the punter did to Crystal, but I heard her scream. Freddie ran upstairs. I heard him shouting, 'Why did you kill him?' I couldn't hear what Crystal replied. I was curious. I crept up the stairs. 'You stupid tart,' Freddie was saying. 'We'll need to get rid of the body. I don't want the police

around here. I've got the half of *Debrett's* downstairs.' I heard
him coming to the door of the room, so I nipped back downstairs. I don't know what they did with the body. After that,
Crystal told me she was getting out of the life. The next thing
I knew was six months later when she invited me to her wedding in the Chelsea registry office. A year later, one of the
girls told me she had bumped into Crystal. She said Crystal
had gone all tweedy and respectable. Crystal told her she was
divorced and was going somewhere to start a new life and
where nothing from her past could catch up with her. I should
have known it was a lie when she told me she was having an
affair. There's nothing like being a working girl to put you off
men for life."

"You'll need to make a sworn statement," said Hamish.

"Will my past life come out? I've gone respectable, and I
don't want the neighbours to know."

"I'll try to keep it quiet. A detective will be calling on you
soon. Don't run away again, or they'll find you. And do not
contact Mrs. Barret-Wilkinson, or we will arrest you. What
was her name before she married?"

"Crystal Jackson."

Hamish drove back to the airport, left the rented car, and
caught the plane to Inverness. He had a sudden idea of how
to clear up the murders, get back at Blair, and avoid any threat
of promotion at the same time.

He had the tape with him in the Land Rover. In his pocket
was a powerful little tape recorder. He had recorded everything Bella had said.

He went to police headquarters in Inverness and asked to speak to Inspector Gannon.

He had to wait some time before she appeared. "What is it?" she asked harshly. "Come to gloat?"

Hamish smiled. "How would you like to get your own back?"

In an interview room, Mary Gannon listened in growing excitement as Hamish described all he had found out about Crystal Barret-Wilkinson. She listened to his taped interview with Bella and then took him to another room with a video player and watched the tape.

At last, she said, "It's enough to get a warrant to search her house. But it's still pretty circumstantial. If she gets a good lawyer, she could walk free or at least get a 'not proven' verdict."

"I have a suggestion to make," said Hamish. "It might just work . . ."

Mrs. Barret-Wilkinson opened the door and looked haughtily at the tall policeman. "What is it now, Officer? It's ten o'clock in the evening."

"I'd better come in," said Hamish. "I have come to accuse you of the murders of Mrs. Gillespie and Shona Fraser."

"You're mad. Oh, come in. This is rubbish."

In her sitting room, Hamish removed his cap and sat down and regarded her steadily.

"Well?" she demanded.

"You'd best sit down."

She sat down in a chair facing him.

"We have a videotape from Trant Television which shows you working as a madam at a club in Beauchamp Place in London. I also have this interview with Bella Robinson."

She listened while he played the tape, the many rings on her fingers digging into her clenched hands.

"So," she said when the tape finished, "I was a tart managing tarts, and it was a long time ago. I had nothing to do with the murders. The professor has confessed."

"Not to the murders, he hasn't," said Hamish. "Mrs. Gillespie recognised you from the television programme and blackmailed you. You've had a lot of luck. Not at first, mind. I think you tried to run her down, but that didn't work, so you followed her to Moy Hall to the clay pigeon shoot and tried to kill her there. You found out her schedule and simply waited outside the professor's for her. Maybe you'd decided to try to talk her out of it or even threaten her to keep quiet. Whatever she said drove you into a mad rage, and you struck her down with her bucket. Then Shona Fraser called on you. Maybe she'd just decided to go around everyone and do a bit of detecting on her own. She, too, recognised you. Maybe you heard her outside phoning me on her mobile. You drove towards Lochdubh. Maybe you'd seen that Land Rover parked up on the hill."

"What Land Rover?"

"Geordie McArthur's."

"Never heard of him."

Hamish experienced a twinge of doubt. He felt she was telling the truth.

"Okay. So you used your own car. Maybe you hid in the

shadows by the police station until you saw her arrive, then you struck her down. You dragged her over to push her into the water, but the body fell into a rowing boat. You went down the stairs, but maybe you heard someone and cut the painter and let the boat drift off."

Hamish saw uneasily that she was beginning to relax.

"And you have forensic proof to back up all your wild imaginings?"

"We'll get it. We'll search this place from top to bottom."

"Let me get this straight. You say you've come here to ar-rest me for two murders, but you are only a village constable. There are no high-ranking police officers, no detectives. Is this flight of fancy all your own?"

Hamish shuffled his boots. "It iss like this. I haff been working on my own. But I haff enough here to start a full investigation. It would save time if you came quietly."

"Oh, I may as well come with you to police headquarters and show you up for the fool you are."

She went over to the table where her handbag lay. She opened it and whipped out a gun and pointed it at Hamish.

She laughed. "You should learn not to confront criminals on your own."

"So you did the murders?" Hamish regarded her steadily.

"Yes, I did, but you're never going to prove it because you aren't going to walk out of here alive."

She shot Hamish Macbeth full in the chest and watched with satisfaction as he keeled over on the floor.

Chapter Ten

He was amazed how so impotent and grovelling insect as I
(these were his expressions) could entertain such inhuman ideas.

—Jonathan Swift

Crystal Barret-Wilkinson kicked Hamish's body savagely with
her foot. "Now I've got to figure out how to get rid of you,"
she said aloud. "I can't go on being lucky. I could hardly believe no one had seen me when I bashed that nosy researcher.
God, I need a drink."

She put down the gun and went to a side table laden with
bottles.

Then she screamed as her arms were wrenched behind her
back and handcuffed. Mary Gannon cautioned her for the
murders of Mrs. Gillespie and Shona Fraser. She had already
telephoned for reinforcements.

Hamish's idea had been that Mary come in the back door
of the house and stand listening as he tried to get a confession
out of Crystal.

Now Hamish Macbeth was dead, and Inspector Gannon would have a hell of a lot of explaining to do.

She thrust Crystal down into a chair and stood over her. "Stay where you are, you murdering bitch, until reinforcements arrive."

Crystal subsided meekly, and then suddenly her booted foot lashed out and caught Mary full in the stomach. Mary doubled over with pain and fell to her knees.

And then Crystal heard a movement. Hamish Macbeth was getting unsteadily to his feet. She let out a scream of pure terror and ran for the door.

Hamish followed in pursuit. Despite the Kevlar bulletproof vest he had been wearing—he had borrowed it from Inverness police headquarters while Mary was getting ready—the blow from the bullet had hurt like hell. He felt unsteady on his legs.

Crystal fled down the road and onto the beach. She cast one anguished look behind her and ran straight into the sea, her wrists still handcuffed. Tearing off his sweater and vest while he ran, Hamish ran into the water after her. A Sutherland gale was blowing and whipping spray from the white crests of the waves into his eyes.

He reached Crystal as she was plunging under the water and caught hold of her. She struggled and fought. He drew back his fist and socked her on the jaw and then dragged her unconscious body back to the shore.

Mary came running down the beach to join him. "Is she dead?"

"No, she'll do," said Hamish. "I had to knock her out."

"How did you survive that shot? I thought you were dead."

"I borrowed a bulletproof vest. But God, that shot made me feel sick."

"We've a lot of explaining to do," said Mary. "Them in Strathbane won't like me poaching on their territory and making them look like fools."

"They'll have to live with it. I've got some dry clothes in the Land Rover," said Hamish. "I'd better get them on."

Crystal began to come round. A stream of filthy oaths emerged from her mouth.

"Here they come," said Mary. She unclipped her torch and flashed it.

Police cars screeched to a halt in front of the beach.

Blair was the first out. He came stumbling down the beach, his heavy face contorted with fury.

"What's all this about?" he shouted. He confronted Mary. "And what are you doing on my patch?"

Fortunately he was followed by Superintendent Daviot. "Let me handle this," he said. "Explain yourself, Inspector."

Crystal was still letting out a stream of curses. "Take her into custody," said Mary. "She is responsible for the deaths of Mrs. Gillespie and Shona Fraser, and we have all the proof you need. She also shot Macbeth, but he was wearing a bulletproof vest."

Daviot gave instructions to police officers who had joined them, and Crystal, kicking and screaming, was dragged off towards the police cars. Jimmy Anderson now joined them.

"It's like this," said Mary, trying to remember the story she had rehearsed with Hamish. "I was checking security at

Inverness airport when I saw Constable Macbeth getting off a Glasgow plane. He told me he had been to Glasgow to check on Mrs. Barret-Wilkinson's alibi."

Her calm, steady voice went on until Daviot had all the facts.

"What I want to know," raged Blair when she finished, "is what this highland loon was doing going to Glasgow without permission?"

"You wouldn't have given me permission," said Hamish. "You would have said that her alibi had already been covered by Strathclyde police."

"Let's get off this beach," said Daviot. "Good work, Hamish, and good work, Inspector."

Back at police headquarters, Hamish, after he had typed out his statement, said to Mary, "I'll be off."

"It's your show. Don't you want to sit in on the interrogation?"

"I'd rather leave it all to you, Inspector."

Hamish drove happily back to Lochdubh. He felt as if a dark cloud of menace had been lifted from the whole Sutherland area.

He called at Angela's and told her and her husband the whole story. "You'd better let me have a look at you," said Dr. Brodie.

Hamish lifted up his sweater. "A nasty bruise, and it'll look worse by tomorrow," the doctor said. He prodded around. "No, no broken ribs. You're a lucky man."

"I know. If she'd shot higher or lower, I might not be here now."

Hamish collected his dog and cat and drove the short distance to the police station.

Home, he thought. Safe home.

He cooked himself a meal of sausage and bacon, ignoring Lugs's insistent paw on his knee and the yellow glare from Sonsie, sitting up on a kitchen chair opposite.

Then he undressed, washed, and fell into bed and straight into a long and dreamless sleep.

A hammering on the kitchen door awoke him late the next morning. He struggled out of bed, put on his dressing gown, and went to answer it. A furious Elspeth stood there with Luke behind her.

"Why didn't you phone me?" she shouted. "We've been to a press conference in Strathbane, and we've only got what all the other papers have. You've just used me as you've used me before as a sort of Watson. I never want to see you or speak to you again!"

She stormed off, deaf to Hamish's apologies. Luke followed. He turned at one point and gave Hamish a mocking smile.

Elspeth and Luke drove back to Strathbane to see if they could pick up any more information before driving to Styre to get the reaction from the few locals.

Luke then suggested they should go back into Strathbane and treat themselves to a slap-up meal at the Palace Hotel.

They had cocktails and then a bottle of wine each to go with their lunch. Elspeth usually didn't drink so much, but she wanted to drown out the pain of what she saw as Hamish Macbeth's cynical and self-seeking behaviour.

Luke set himself out to be charming and amusing. He told Elspeth she was the most attractive woman he had ever met. Tipsy, and feeling happier, Elspeth reflected that Hamish had never said one nice word about her appearance. On the contrary, he usually criticised what she had on.

Over coffee and large brandies, Luke reached over the table and took her hand in his.

"We make a good team, Elspeth," he said. He rose and got down on one knee beside her chair. Still holding her hand, he looked up into her face and said, "Beautiful Elspeth, light of my life, will you marry me?"

The other diners fell silent. Elspeth thought of her lonely flat back in Glasgow. She thought about how stupid she'd been to ever have fancied such as Hamish Macbeth.

"Yes," she said.

The diners cheered. Luke rose and pulled her to her feet. "Let's go and get the best ring Strathbane has to offer."

Unbeknownst to them, Hamish Macbeth had just left the main jewellers' shop before they arrived, a sapphire and diamond ring in his pocket. He had at last decided that if marriage was what Elspeth wanted, then marriage was what she would get. As he drove back to Lochdubh, he conjured up happy pictures of Elspeth working in his kitchen with a small son at her heels.

But when he arrived at the Tommel Castle Hotel, there was no sign of Elspeth. He mooched around, getting more and more anxious as the day wore on, until Mr. Johnson invited him into his office. "Sit down and have a coffee. You can see the car park from the window."

Hamish sat down. He took out the ring in its little red leather box and flicked the lid up and down until Mr. Johnson told him to stop it. "She's out reporting, that's all, Hamish."

"Did I tell you why she was mad at me?"

"Only about a hundred times," said Mr. Johnson, then hearing the sound of car wheels on the gravel outside, he added, "Someone's arriving."

Hamish went to the window, and Mr. Johnson joined him. Elspeth and Luke got out. They were both laughing at something. Then Luke took Elspeth in his arms and kissed her. She put her hands up to caress the back of his neck, and one last ray of bright sunlight sparkled on a large diamond ring on her finger.

Hamish made for the door, but the manager held him back.

"Leave it, Hamish. There's nothing you can do now."

Back at the police station, Hamish found Inspector Mary Gannon waiting for him. "I'm off back to Inverness," she said. "I dropped by to thank you. Blair's in the doghouse again with Daviot for having decided the prof was the villain."

"Come ben," said Hamish. "Drink?"

"No, I'm driving."

"Tea?"

"That would be grand."

"The thing that amazed me," said Hamish as he waited for the kettle to boil, "is the luck of the woman! I mean, if I walked down the waterfront here at two in the morning, at least five people would ask me the next day what I was doing at that time of night. No one saw her at the professor's, yet when I park at the end of his street, the neighbours report me."

"I think," said Mary, "that if she hadn't been such an amateur, we might have caught her. I know it sounds daft, but the chances she took! And nearly got away with it."

"When's the court case?"

"Sometime in February at the High Court in Edinburgh. You'll be informed. You'll need to be a witness for the prosecution. She got herself a top advocate—but too late, because, in a mad rage, she told us at the interview exactly how she had done the murders. I think her advocate will try for a plea of insanity. Scotland Yard are investigating that murder in the brothel that Bella talked about."

"Crystal must have really craved respectability. Help yourself to milk and sugar. I've got biscuits somewhere. Did she confess to frightening Mrs. Samson to death after trying to set her house on fire?"

"Yes."

"How did she know about the package that Mrs. Gillespie left for Mrs. Samson?"

"I love this one. Blair went to interview her some days after the fire, and they got very cosy. He told her about it. Of course, he's denying the whole thing. No biscuits for me. Tea is fine. You're a waste of a good detective, Macbeth."

"Can you see me in Strathbane, taking orders from Blair?" asked Hamish. "I'm king and emperor of my own patch here. When things are quiet, it's a grand life."

"I know you must be feeling a certain amount of delayed shock," said Mary, studying his face. "But you've got a miserable sort of haunted look in your eyes."

Hamish found himself telling her all about how he had hoped to propose to Elspeth but had been pipped at the post by Luke.

"That's bad. Had you known her long?"

"Yes, quite a bit."

"Why didn't you ask her before?"

"I think I was in love with someone else."

She laughed. "You think? Let me tell you something. I think you were, or are, suffering from delayed shock. It's not every day you nearly get killed. I think you wanted security. You're a man. You wanted comforting sex. It wouldn't surprise me if you've forgotten the whole thing by tomorrow."

"I'll never forget her," said Hamish stubbornly, then, switching subjects, added, "I thought you were going to resign when the case was over."

"I changed my mind. They're a nice crowd in Inverness. I've bought you a present."

"There was no need for that. What is it?"

"A joiner will call on you tomorrow and fix a cat flap in that door. It'll be big enough for your dog as well. It comes with bolts so you can fasten it securely when the animals don't need to use it."

"That's right kind of you."

Mary finished her tea. "Call on me if you're ever in Inverness."

After Mary had left, Hamish walked along to Patel's and bought himself some cold ham, liver for Lugs, and a fresh fish from the harbour for Sonsie. He fed the animals first and then added fried eggs to the cold ham for himself. He made a pot of tea and carried the lot into the living room. He set the tray on the floor, raked out the fire and lit it, switched on the television, and watched the news while he ate.

The arrest of Crystal had made the headlines. There was Daviot speaking at the press conference and giving all the praise to Inspector Gannon while Blair glowered in the background. Hamish was not mentioned, which, he thought, suited him fine.

The news was followed by a drama. He put his tray on the floor after he had finished eating and settled back to watch. Sonsie jumped on his lap, but he put the heavy cat down. "You're a wild cat," said Hamish. "Behave like one."

Gradually his eyelids drooped, and he fell asleep.

He awoke with a start later. The fire had burnt down to red ash. The cat was back on his lap, and her weight had given him pins and needles in his legs. He rose and carried his tray of dishes through to the kitchen. He put the dishes in the sink, poured water on them, and left them to soak. Hamish thought the two best housekeeping excuses in the world were leaving the dishes to soak and the beds to air.

It was only when he was undressed and lying in bed that he realised he was not thinking of Elspeth. The whole business of wanting to propose to her seemed like a dream.

A blessedly crime-free autumn moved into winter. A series of very hard frosts gripped the countryside. Quite often, Sutherland—the south land of the old Vikings—escapes the worst of the winter because of the proximity of the Gulf Stream. But as Christmas passed and the New Year dawned, a raging blizzard struck the Highlands. It came unexpectedly, for the day had started off fine and frosty.

Hamish was returning from Patel's with a bag of groceries when he noticed a bank of black clouds looming up in the north. He walked to the wall and stared out over the loch. The air was very still, and yet those clouds advanced across the sky. The first flakes of snow soon began to fall, lacy flakes spiralling down and then upwards on the frosty air. The wind began to blow, and the snow thickened. Hypnotised, he watched the advance of the clouds as the wind blew harder. He could understand why, in the olden days, people thought the god Thor rode the gales with his army.

He turned and headed for the police station, dropped his groceries on the table, got bales of winter feed out of the shed, and set off up the hill to his small flock of sheep. He herded them into a shelter he had built the previous spring and watched them as they fed before he turned and hurried back through the yelling, screeching wind. Thor and his army had arrived over Lochdubh. The noise of the storm was deafening.

The cat flap banged, and Sonsie and then Lugs appeared. He got a towel and rubbed each of them down.

There was nothing he could do now but wait until the blizzard died down.

The morning dawned sunny and frosty, but a gale was still blowing powdery snow off the tops of the drifts.

The snowplough passed the window of the police station, followed by a lorry spraying grit and salt.

Hamish had snow tyres on his Land Rover, something he had campaigned for and had finally got.

He decided to see if he could get up to the Strathbane road to find out how Geordie McArthur was doing and then, maybe, visit some more of the outlying crofts.

The road up to Geordie's from the main road was impassable, so he strapped on his snowshoes and set out.

Geordie answered the door, his face flushed with whisky and bad temper.

"Get lost," he snarled.

Hamish stood his ground.

"How's the missus?"

"She left me afore Christmas to stay with her sister in Bonar Bridge. The minister's wife got hold o' her and she became that uppity, so I gave her a taste o' ma belt and the next day herself was gone. She's filing for a divorce. The minister's wife told me you were concerned, so it's all your fault, you bampot. Get the hell out o' here."

Hamish turned away. Some sixth sense made him duck as a large boot sailed over his head. Now, I could arrest him for that, thought Hamish, but just think of the paperwork. He plodded on through the drifts to his vehicle. Another blizzard was now screeching across the countryside.

Nothing more he could do but return to the police station and read books and watch television.

After a night and day of pure white hell, the snow stopped falling and the wind died.

The following day was bright and sunny. Hamish shovelled snow, fed his sheep and hens, and did chores around his home.

The snowplough and the gritter had cleared a path along the waterfront. By evening, Hamish decided to reward himself by going to the Italian restaurant for a decent meal.

He put Sonsie in a haversack on his back and carried Lugs in his arms. He knew the salt on the road would hurt the animals' paws.

Willie Lamont, the waiter, greeted him with delight. "This weather!" he exclaimed. "I thought I'd never see another customer again. I'll take the beasties into the kitchen. This snow! It's a fair cats trophy."

"*Catastrophe*," corrected Hamish, sitting down at a table by the window. "You'll have plenty of folks in here soon. Patel's grocery will soon be running out of stores. How are you doing yourselves?"

"We've enough pasta in the storeroom to feed the whole o' Italy, and we've got a deer for the Bolognese sauce and things. Once the venison's ground up and put in the sauce, folks can't tell the difference."

"How did you get the deer?" asked Hamish suspiciously.

"The poor thing just dropped dead outside the kitchen door. Must have been the cold."

Or the quick slash of a kitchen knife, thought Hamish cynically. Willie went off to the kitchen, with Sonsie and Lugs trotting eagerly at his heels.

The door opened, letting in a blast of cold air. A vision entered the restaurant. She was tall and blonde and wearing a white quilted anorak with a fur-lined hood.

She smiled at Hamish. "What weather!" Her voice had a slight trace of a foreign accent.

"Visiting?" asked Hamish.

"Yes, I'm staying at the hotel. I thought I'd never get out. May I join you?"

"Of course."

She took off her anorak and hung it on a peg by the door. She was wearing a white cashmere dress with a white cashmere cardigan. Round her neck was a rope of pearls. She had perfect skin, very white, high cheekbones, and green eyes. Her mouth was full and sensuous.

She sat down gracefully opposite Hamish. "Are you visiting?" she asked.

"No, I live here. I'm the local policeman."

She gave a tinkling laugh. "I didn't think there were any local policemen left in Britain."

Hamish grinned. "I hang on. I like being an anachronism. It's an odd time to visit the Highlands."

"Oh, I'd never been to Scotland before. I live in London."

"My name is Hamish Macbeth."

"And mine is Gloria Price."

"Staying long?"

"Just a week."

"Are you on your own?"

"Completely." She picked up the menu. "Seems to be a lot of venison. I think I'll stick to pasta."

Willie came rushing out. "Good evening, madam," he said. "We have plenty of tables, and Mr. Macbeth may be waiting for Miss Halburton-Smythe."

"I am not waiting for anyone," said Hamish, irritated, knowing that Willie, like many of the locals, had never forgiven him for breaking off his engagement to Priscilla. "Take the order."

Both ordered minestrone. Gloria chose lasagne to follow, and Hamish did the same.

"Would you choose the wine?" asked Gloria.

Hamish ordered a bottle of Valpolicella.

After Willie had retreated, Hamish asked, "What is your job?"

Again that charming laugh. "I don't work. I am independently wealthy."

"Ah, your husband is successful?"

She waved her fingers at him. "See, no wedding ring? The money is all mine. Daddy has shops all over the place."

"What kind of shops?"

"Electrical goods, washing machines, computers, all that sort of stuff."

"But you must have been married."

"Never could find the right man. Of course, a lot of men have fancied my money. Tell me about your job."

"It's very quiet now," said Hamish. "A few break-ins, nothing special."

"But I read in the newspapers about murders up here."

"Ah, fortunately that's all over and done with."

"Tell me about it."

Hamish had the highlander's gift of telling a good story, perhaps because the north of Scotland is the last place on earth where someone can tell a long story without fear of interruption.

Gloria was a good listener, and by the end of the meal, Hamish realised guiltily that he had been talking during the whole meal about himself.

He insisted on paying.

"I must return some of this hospitality," she said. "Why don't you come back with me to the hotel for a nightcap?"

"That would be grand, but I've got my dog and cat in the kitchen. If you go on ahead, I'll follow you."

Willie came out of the kitchen, followed by the cat and dog. Hamish was helping Gloria into her coat.

Sonsie glared at Gloria, her lips drawn back in a snarl and her fur on end. Lugs let out a sharp bark.

"What's got into you?" shouted Hamish. He opened the door and ushered Gloria out. "I won't be long," he said to her.

"I've told you and told you," complained Willie, "that you shouldn't be keeping a wild cat. That animal'll kill someone one of these days."

Hamish lifted up the cat and put her in his haversack, then picked up Lugs. "You're a right jealous pair," he lectured.

He took them back to the police station and left them in the kitchen before climbing into the Land Rover and heading up through the white walls of snow on either side of the road to the hotel.

He felt intrigued and happy at the same time. For a moment, Elspeth's image hung in his brain like a pale ghost, and then it was gone.

Gloria was waiting for him in the reception area. She rose and walked forward to meet him. "There's a noisy shinty team celebrating in the bar," she said. "Let's go up to my room. I've got a good bottle of malt."

To his surprise, she led the way along a corridor past the manager's office. "You've hired the bridal suite," exclaimed Hamish.

"I like my comfort," she said over her shoulder, "and I like to be on the ground floor."

The suite consisted of a pretty sitting room and a double bedroom. "Make yourself comfortable," said Gloria. "How do you take your whisky? Straight?"

"Just with a splash of water and not too much. I've got to drive back."

She picked up a bottle from a side table. "Take a look out of the window, Hamish. Is it still blocked with that drift? I asked them to clear it."

Hamish went to the window. "Pretty clear," he said.

He sat down on a sofa. She sat opposite him in an armchair. "Cheers," she said, smiling at him over her raised glass.

"Cheers." Hamish took a sip, thinking she really had a beautiful face, thinking suddenly he had seen that face before.

She put down her glass. "I'm just going to repair my make-up. Won't be a moment."

Hamish was beginning to feel dizzy. He'd only had one sip. What the hell had she put in his drink? He knew now where he'd seen her—on that grainy video of the brothel. She had been one of the girls.

Freddie Ionedes had gone missing. Was she still working for him?

He decided to play along. He nipped over to the window, raised it, poured the rest of the drink in the snow, dived back to the sofa, slumped down, and closed his eyes just as she came out of the bathroom.

He felt her standing over him, smelled her perfume, sensed instinctively that she was going to do something to make sure he was really unconscious. When she slapped him hard across the face, he nearly betrayed himself, but instead he allowed his body to sag sideways on the sofa. He heard her make a phone call. "All set," she whispered.

Then he heard the window being raised. Sounds of someone climbing in. A man's voice said, "Good girl. Let's get moving."

Gloria's voice: "Do we have to do this, Freddie?"

"I look after my own. Crystal wants him dead, and dead he's going to be. No one will suspect anything. Did anyone see him coming into the hotel?"

"No, the reception was empty when he arrived."

"Murphy's outside, dressed in police uniform. He's hotwired the Land Rover. He's bringing it round to the window. We'll get this pillock out and into the back of the Land Rover. I'll follow. Murphy knows where to go. If anyone sees him, they'll think it's this fool. All we do is lay him out in the snow, tip the Land Rover on its side. It'll look as if he's been thrown out. He'll die in the cold before he ever gets a chance to come round. Tragic accident. You stay here and act the perfect guest."

"I thought the reception was empty," Gloria said, "but what if someone saw him come in? He isn't in uniform."

"Then say he got called out. He went back to the station to put his uniform on. You stay on here and act the perfect guest," Freddie repeated.

Hamish recognised the sound of his Land Rover.

He heard Freddie say, "Climb in, Murphy. I'll need your help getting him out."

Hamish found it an effort to lie like a dead weight as he was shoved out of the window and into the snow. Then he was heaved into the back of his Land Rover.

As they drove off, Hamish cautiously slid his mobile phone out of his pocket. He texted Jimmy. Then he punched in Angela's number, and when she answered, he whispered, "Hamish here. Danger. Freddie Ionedes is trying to kill me. Tell Strathbane. Set up roadblocks."

He had been trying for ages to get a new Land Rover. Now he was glad of its age and the noisy engine that had drowned out the sound of his whispered voice.

As he had guessed, they only drove a comparatively short way. They wouldn't want to get lost on the moors. They would stage the accident just off the main road, as the side roads were still banked up with drifts.

The Land Rover stopped. Hamish was dragged out and carried to a deep drift at the side of the road and thrown in.

"Shall we tip the Rover over on him?" he heard Murphy ask.

"No, I don't want a mark on him."

Hamish poked a finger upwards to give himself a breathing hole in the drift. He heard them panting and struggling as they tried to tip the Land Rover on its side.

"It's no use," came Freddie's voice. "Leave it. Let's get out of here."

The cold was intense. Hamish fought against it. He did not want to die of cold after having survived this far.

To his relief, he heard them driving off.

He rose out of the snowdrift and climbed into the Land Rover, fishing for his keys and hoping the hot-wiring hadn't messed up the engine. But the old vehicle roared to life. He turned the heater on full blast. He guessed they would take the road to Strathbane and then off down south. He set off in pursuit.

Freddie and Murphy were laughing as they drove slowly through the white wilderness. "I'm telling you, I'm a genius," said Freddie. "Can't you go any faster?"

"The night's so cold that the grit isn't doing much. We'll skid if we go any faster," said Murphy.

Murphy negotiated a corner and then swore. An old car was blocking the road.

"Come on," said Freddie. "Get out and help me move it."

They both approached the car and began to try to push it to the side of the road.

Suddenly they were surrounded by a ring of men holding shotguns. "Get down on the ground," shouted Willie Lamont.

Freddie reached inside his parka for his gun and was felled with the butt of a shotgun. Murphy whimpered with terror.

Hamish Macbeth came driving up to a cheer from the men. He climbed down and handcuffed Murphy and cautioned him and then handcuffed the prone body of Freddie.

The pair were taken down to the police station and locked in the cell. Hamish changed into his uniform and sent for Dr. Brodie to examine Freddie, who was showing signs of coming round.

"He'll have a big lump, and he'll suffer from concussion," said Dr. Brodie. "But he'll live."

Willie Lamont, the waiter who had once been in the police force, came in with Gloria.

"Shove her in the cell," said Hamish. "The heavy mob'll be along soon."

Freddie recovered full consciousness and began to swear. Hamish charged him with attempted murder, kidnapping, and carrying a firearm. He then turned and charged Gloria with aiding and abetting kidnapping and attempted murder.

"He made me do it!" cried Gloria, her face streaked with tears.

Hamish ignored her. He ushered Dr. Brodie out of the cell and turned and locked it.

"Here they come," said Dr. Brodie as the wail of sirens grew nearer.

"I'll be glad to get rid of them," said Hamish.

It was a long night. Hamish had to follow the triumphant cavalcade of police vehicles to Strathbane, triumphant because the Northern Constabulary felt they had captured a dangerous criminal where Scotland Yard had failed.

His eyes gritty with fatigue, Hamish typed out a long statement. Then he was tested to find out what sort of drug had been put in his drink, although he complained that there was probably ample evidence of it somewhere in Gloria's hotel room. Then he was interrogated by Daviot.

"If only you had married Miss Halburton-Smythe," said Daviot after Hamish had finished his account, "you would not be easy prey to every harpy who crosses your path."

"You've got your man, sir, and you wouldn't have got him if he hadn't come after me. And there's one thing. That Land Rover of mine needs to be replaced. I cover a fair bit of the north of Scotland. What if it breaks down on an important job?"

"We'll see what we can do. It'll need to stay here while the forensic team go over it. I'll get a constable to drive you home. Have you typed up your report?"

"Yes, sir."

"I don't think we'll be needing you further. Mr. Blair and I will do the interrogation. Some officers from Scotland Yard will be arriving tomorrow."

And Blair doesn't want me around to steal any of the glory, thought Hamish cynically.

A pretty police constable was waiting for him. She had a mop of black curly hair and a rosy face. "Pat Constable," she said.

"Pat what?"

"Constable. And spare me the jokes."

"Been on the force long?"

"Only a few months."

He leaned back in the seat of the police car, glad to be going home at last. He would have liked to sleep, but Pat kept asking him questions about the events of the night and Hamish found he was so bored with the sound of his own voice going over the whole thing again that he could have screamed.

As he got out stiffly from the car, highland courtesy demanded that he offer the constable some refreshment, and to his dismay, she accepted. He hoped his cat would take one of its rare dislikes to her and frighten her off, but Pat was intrigued by Sonsie and made such a fuss of the animal that the cat's deep purrs reverberated around the kitchen.

Hamish made tea and produced a tin of biscuits. Pat had just come on the night shift and was as bright as a button. She told him all about her family in Dornoch, about her time at the police academy, while Hamish stifled his yawns and sent prayers up to the old Celtic gods to make her go.

At last, she rose to leave. "Maybe we could have dinner together one evening," she said.

"Aye, maybe," said Hamish, resisting an urge to put his hand in the small of her back and shove her out the door.

She turned out to be one of those irritating people who get up to leave and then stand in the doorway chattering away.

She finally left. He sighed with relief. He walked like a zombie into his bedroom, fell facedown on the bed, and collapsed into a dreamless sleep.

Hamish was awakened at ten the next morning by a loud hammering at the front door.

I'm not going to answer that, he thought. Probably the press. The knocking grew louder, and a voice shouted, "Scotland Yard. Open up."

Groaning, Hamish went to the front door and shouted through the letter box, "Come round to the kitchen door. This one's jammed with the damp."

He went to the kitchen door and opened it, suddenly sharply aware of his unshaven face and scruffy clothes as two smartly dressed men wearing expensive parkas over their suits came round the corner.

"Police Constable Hamish Macbeth?"

"That's me."

"I am Detective Chief Inspector Burrows from Scotland Yard, and this is Detective Sergeant Wilkins."

"Come ben," said Hamish. "I'm just up. It was a long night. I'll make up the stove."

Burrows watched with some amusement as Hamish raked out the stove, put paper and kindling in it, and struck a match. He had sensed in talking to Daviot and Blair that the detective abilities of Hamish Macbeth were being kept out of the picture, and he had decided to see the man for himself. He saw a tall, sleepy highlander with flaming red hair and almost guileless hazel eyes.

"Please sit down," said Hamish, adding slabs of peat to the blaze. "Tea?"

"We've brought our own supplies," said Burrows, lifting a carrier back onto the table. "We've a couple of thermoses of coffee and some croissants. And a bottle of whisky."

"That was really thoughtful of ye," said Hamish. "Where did you get croissants in Strathbane?"

"I gather it's a new bakery."

"Won't last," said Hamish. "They prefer things like deep-fried Mars bars."

They all sat round the table. Burrows was a clean-cut man with neat features, while his sergeant was large with a great round head.

"What we would like," said Burrows, "is to hear your version of events, starting with the murder cases. My God! What the hell's that? A lynx?"

"That's my cat," said Hamish patiently. "Please may I have some coffee, and no, I don't want any whisky in it."

He began at the beginning again. Although he tried hard to make it look as if he had been nothing more than a bumbling local policeman who had hit upon clues by sheer accident, Burrows was not deceived.

After Hamish had finished, Burrows said, "I think you should be due for a promotion."

He was startled by the look of alarm on Hamish's face. "Who iss talking about promotion?" asked Hamish nervously.

"None of them at Strathbane. But I was going to put in a recommendation."

"Please don't do that, sir."

Wilkins spoke for the first time. "He likes it here, sir. I like it here. I've been looking out the window at the sheep. I like looking at sheep."

"Dear me. A country boy at heart? Is he right, Macbeth?"

"Aye. You see, you need a village policeman in this part o' the world. If I got a promotion, they would shut down this police station. The folks from Strathbane would never think of checking on the old folks in the outlying crofts. They talk about community policing, but there's damn little of it I can see."

Said Burrows, "You mean you have no ambition what-soever?"

"There iss the one thing."

"And that is?"

"I need a new Land Rover. If you could put a word in for me about that."

"I'll do my best. We'd better get going. It might snow again."

"A thaw is coming."

"How do you know? Seen the weather forecast, have you?"

"No, I can always feel it."

The two Scotland Yard officers drove south to Strathbane. "Look, sir, the snow is melting," said Wilkins.

"Strange man that Macbeth," said Burrows. "He really

needs a good strong push up the ladder. He shouldn't be rotting in a country village."

"He's not rotting, sir," said Wilkins vehemently. "He's
happy. Why is it that no one can stand a happy, contented,
unambitious man?"

Burrows gave a reluctant laugh. "I've never met one before. I
want to change him into one of us. Calm down. I'll leave him
alone."

Chapter 11

The best laid schemes o' mice and men
Gang aft a-gley.

—Robert Burns

Spring came reluctantly to the Highlands, crawling in on sleety gusts of wind. Then one day, the sun shone down from a cloudless sky. The air of Lochdubh was filled with the sound of vacuum cleaners and flapping dusters as the inhabitants got down to the annual spring cleaning.

Hamish Macbeth, now proud possessor of a brand-new Land Rover, felt it was time that he, too, did some spring cleaning.

As he worked away, his mind seemed to be waking up again after the long, cold winter.

He found himself wondering how the one-time suspects in the murder cases were getting on now that they no longer had any fear of the police prying into their private lives.

Thanks to the new cat flap, Sonsie and Lugs could get in

and out of the house whenever they wanted. He left his chores and drove off towards Braikie, marvelling at the glory of the day.

Even the sea along by the shore road was quiet, with only little glassy waves curling on the beach.

His thoughts turned reluctantly to Elspeth. Was she married? Was she happy? Would he ever see her again?

At that moment, Elspeth was arriving at the church in Glasgow in a carriage drawn by two white horses donated by her Gypsy relatives. Beside her sat her uncle Mark, uncomfortable in his wedding finery. The best man, Luke's fellow reporter James Biddell, came up to the carriage. "Drive around again," he said. "Luke hasn't arrived."

"Where is he?" demanded Elspeth.

"We finished up the stag party at four this morning. He said he was going back to his digs. I called round, but he wasn't there."

"I'll murder the bastard," grated Uncle Mark. "Drive on."

If only I had insisted on a closed limo, thought Elspeth. Crowds were gathering to see the bride. By the time they came round to the church again, a procession had formed behind the carriage.

But there was James shaking his head. "You didn't do anything nasty to him?" asked Elspeth. "You didn't tie him up to a lamp post or something?"

"Nothing like that," said James shiftily. How could he tell Elspeth, looking so beautiful in her white wedding gown, that they had hired a stripper for the evening and that drunken Luke had gone off with her?

"I'm getting down," said Elspeth. "I'm not going to make a spectacle of myself, driving round and round."

Groaning and wheezing and complaining that his collar was strangling him, Uncle Mark helped her down and led her into the church.

Elspeth's two bridesmaids were waiting in the church porch. From inside the church came the sound of the organ and the impatient rustling and whispers of the guests.

Gazing out at the blue sky above the grimy Glasgow buildings, Elspeth suddenly wished herself back in the Highlands. Did she really want to marry Luke? Somehow the whole thing had gained momentum: presents from the staff, arrangements for the reception.

Half an hour passed. Elspeth turned to her uncle. "Get in there and tell them the wedding's cancelled but they can all go on to the reception and get something to eat and drink."

"Don't worry, lass. We'll hunt him down and drag him to the altar."

"I won't marry him after this," said Elspeth. "Get on with the announcement."

So the announcement was made, and the guests made their way out to the cars. Elspeth refused to get back into the carriage and shared a car with her editor. What a mess! They were due to leave on their honeymoon that very day. Luke had the air tickets to Barbados.

The reception, fuelled by good food and a lot of drink, turned out to be a noisy affair. After the meal, Elspeth took the floor for the first dance with James. She felt suddenly very happy and relieved. She realised with a shock that she had been dreading this wedding, dreading being married to Luke.

Luke awoke with a groan and stared up at a dingy, unfamiliar ceiling. He rolled over and collided with a body in the bed next to him. "Elspeth?" he said.

The woman next to him opened eyes heavy with mascara and stared at him.

"Who are you?" asked Luke.

"Well, that's a nice thing. You screw me and then ask who I am?"

Luke swung his legs out of the bed and clutched his head, which felt as if all the hammers of hell were beating inside his skull.

Memory came back in bright little cameos. He remembered the stripper. He remembered betting the lads that he could lay her.

"What's the time?" he asked groggily.

"Dunno."

He twisted round and found his watch on a bedside table. "Oh, my God, I was due at the church two hours ago."

"Then you'd better get there," said the stripper sulkily.

"It's too late. Those relatives of hers will kill me! I'll get the sack."

Luke got dressed. He checked his pocket for his wallet and found it was intact along with a book of traveller's cheques and two tickets to Barbados.

His one thought now was escape. He stumbled out onto

the balcony and found himself high up in a tower block. He peered over the railing, and stretched out below him was the depressed area of Springburn.

The lift wasn't working. He ran down the stairs and down the hill to the Springburn road, where, wonder upon wonders, a cab came cruising along. He hailed it. "Airport," he said breathlessly. "As fast as you can make it."

Hamish was irritated that his thoughts kept returning to Elspeth. She was probably married now, he thought crossly. She might even be pregnant.

He halted in front of St. Mary's Church. Father McNulty was just leaving the church. He smiled when he saw Hamish.

"I called to find out if you ever got that money back," said Hamish.

"Oh, yes, Miss Creedy sold her shop and paid me back. It was kind of you to keep it quiet."

"To tell the truth, Father, I was glad of the horrible winter for one reason—it stopped her haunting me."

"I don't think the lady will be haunting you again. Miss Creedy has moved to Glasgow. I had a letter from her the other day. She seemed very happy and said she had a gentleman friend. I really cannot understand such as Mrs. Gillespie, nor can I understand how she found people with so many guilty secrets in the one area."

"We all of us have guilty secrets, Father, and here in the north, people still prize respectability. That, too, was the downfall of our murderess. Maybe she sometimes came across one of her clients out on the London streets with his family and saw the way his eyes averted when he saw her. The irony of it is that maybe one of the wives saw her and thought, I would like to be as beautiful as that, while Crystal was jealously thinking, if only I could get out of the life and be dull and respectable."

"She did not look very beautiful to judge from her photograph in the newspapers."

"She was once, but she had put on weight and become tweedy and matronly. Tell me, Father, do you sometimes wonder why someone as young as Shona should be so brutally killed?"

"You mean, why should God let such a thing happen?"

"Yes."

"That way madness lies. The only answer is blind faith. There are children dying all over the world as we speak."

Hamish suddenly felt embarrassed. "I'll be off, then."

His next call was on Mr. Gillespie. Although Heather had told him that her father's cancer was in remission, he wondered whether he was still alive.

But it was a very cheerful Mr. Gillespie who answered the door to him. "Come in," he said. "I was just about to put the kettle on."

The living room was pleasantly cluttered with newspapers and books. As Mr. Gillespie served coffee, Hamish asked, "How are you?"

"I can hardly believe it. I'm in remission. They say it's a miracle."

"I'm right glad for you."

"I think it might be having an end to years of torment."

"You could have reported her."

"It's hard for a man to do that. I didn't think the police would have believed me."

"I would."

"I really didn't know about the blackmail. I really thought her employers were very generous."

"I might go up to the hospital and check on Dr. Renfrew," said Hamish.

"Oh, he's left the area. Someone at the hospital told me he had moved to Edinburgh. His wife is still here. She filed for divorce. My daughter told me it was the talk of Braikie. Mrs. Fleming called at her home and told Mrs. Renfrew she had been having an affair with her husband."

"How did Heather learn this?"

"Someone was passing and witnessed the scene, and soon it was all over the village."

"It's amazing how many people witness things when I don't need a witness," said Hamish crossly.

"What about that man Freddie Ionedes?"

"He got sent away for a long time. It was understood he helped in a murder some time ago, but they haven't any real proof, and the police are satisfied that he's out of society. He left court swearing vengeance on me."

"Well, he can't do anything about that now."

"I'm not so sure," said Hamish. "He was quite an important member of the underworld."

"I'm surprised he was able to run a brothel in a place like Knightsbridge."

"It was described as a drinking club. Important people used

it—members of Parliament, high-ranking police officers, people like that. There will always be a market."

"It's all over now."

"I hope so," said Hamish.

The next few weeks passed pleasantly. The weather was a mixture of showers and sunshine. Hamish drove diligently around his long beat, checking on people in the outlying crofts, drinking tea and gossiping, doing all the things that made him enjoy his job.

And then one morning as he was raking out the stove, there came a knock on the front door. He wiped a grimy hand over his brow, went through, and shouted, "Come to the side door."

He hoped it wasn't someone from Strathbane, come to interrupt his tranquil life.

He opened the door. A tall, slim woman stood there, expensively elegant in a well-tailored trouser suit. Masses of auburn hair framed an attractive face. Wide-spaced brown eyes, high cheekbones, and a beautiful mouth.

"I'm visiting the area," she said. Her voice was pleasant but held traces of cockney. "I wondered if you could tell me the best places around here to visit."

"If you go along to the general store, just inside the door you'll find a rack of tourist brochures," said Hamish. "Where are you from?"

"I'm from London. I read about those murders and saw film of this area on television. It looked so beautiful and I was in need of a holiday, so here I am. I'm staying at the hotel."

"Mr. Johnson, the manager, has plenty of tourist information."

"May I come in?"

"Why?" asked Hamish.

"I've never been inside a country police station before."

"Just for a minute, then." Hamish stood aside to let her past.

She settled herself at the kitchen table. A waft of some subtle perfume emanated from her.

"Would you like tea or coffee?" asked Hamish reluctantly.

"Coffee would be nice."

"Wait until I finish cleaning out the stove."

She sat placidly, seeming perfectly at ease. The cat flap banged, and Lugs followed by Sonsie strolled into the kitchen.

"Is that a . . . ?"

"Yes, it's a wild cat," said Hamish, "but harmless."

She opened her handbag and took out a camera. "Mind if I take a picture?"

"Yes. They don't like having their pictures taken."

"Oh, well, pity."

Hamish finished cleaning the stove and plugged in an electric kettle. He rarely used it, preferring to keep a kettle boiling on the top of the stove, but he thought it would take too long and he wanted rid of her. He did not want a beautiful woman to upset his placid existence.

"My name is Tasman Kennedy," she said.

"I'm Hamish Macbeth. Where does the Scottish name come from?"

"My grandfather was Scottish. But I've never been in Scotland before. When I drove up, I could hardly believe the emptiness. It's so crowded in the south. It's hard to believe there are places like this in the British Isles."

"What do you do for a living?" asked Hamish, putting a mug of coffee in front of her. "Help yourself to milk and sugar."

"I'm a model. Photographic model mostly, although I go on the catwalk for the collections."

"Is it hard work?"

"It is. And I know it's a short life. I don't use drugs like some of the others. Any money I get, I put into property. I may even buy something up here."

"I wouldn't bother. It looks fine at the moment, but the summer is brief and the winters can be hard."

"But you like it."

"Yes, but I'm a highlander. It makes a difference."

She took a sip of her coffee and wrinkled her nose.

"It was on special at Patel's," said Hamish defensively.

"It's nearly lunchtime," she said. "Why don't I take you for lunch at the hotel?"

Hamish stared at her for a long moment, his eyes blank. Then he said, "That would be nice. I'm supposed to be on duty. I'll need to put my uniform on in case someone from headquarters sees me."

During the meal, Hamish's suspicions grew. He had wondered how long it would be before Freddie Ionedes from his prison cell would arrange something horrible for him. He had certainly pulled out all the stops with this one. Tasman was amusing and charming. She told funny stories about her appearances on the catwalk.

Hamish played along, wondering all the while what was in store for him.

And although he smiled and chatted, he could feel himself getting angrier and angrier. No one this beautiful could be interested in such as Hamish Macbeth.

He had an idea. He was not going to go along with it. He was not going to be a sitting duck. What had they planned for him this time? Were they going to take him out to sea in a boat and throw him over? Take him up to a peat bog and drop him in?

Towards the end of the meal, Hamish thanked her with every appearance of warmth and then said, "You didn't get a proper look at the police station. Why not come back with me and I'll show you round."

"I'd like that. But not your coffee. Let's have it here and then we'll go."

Tasman followed Hamish to the police station in her car. He courteously helped her out. The sun was sparkling on the loch. Seagulls sailed overhead. A beautiful schooner cruised out to sea under full sail. No one is going to spoil this for me again, he vowed.

Hamish ushered her inside. "Now you've seen the kitchen. I actually have a cell. Would you like to see it?"

"Yes. Do you lock many people up?"

"Usually only one of the locals who's drunk too much. I

lock the man up and let him out in the morning when he's slept it off. Here it is."

She gave a charming laugh. "It looks quite cosy."

Hamish put a hand in the small of her back and pushed her in. "Take a good look at it from the inside." She staggered forward into the cell, and he banged the door shut and locked it.

She hammered on the door. "Let me out, you maniac!"

Hamish ignored her and went through to the computer. Time to check the police files before he phoned Strathbane.

But before he could get to the office, the Currie sisters walked in. "Where is she?" asked Nessie eagerly.

"Is she," echoed Jessie. "Is that her screaming, screaming?"

"What are you talking about?" demanded Hamish.

"We've only seen her on the telly and in the magazines," said Jessie. "We've never seen a famous model close up."

Colour flooded Hamish's face. "Famous model?" he echoed.

"Yes, the whole village is that excited."

Hamish all but pushed them out the door. "Come back later." He slammed the kitchen door on their startled faces and locked it. Then he went and unlocked the cell.

"I should have known better than to spend time with the village idiot," raged Tasman.

"Before you do that," pleaded Hamish, "let me tell you a story."

"What? About the little people, you inbred moron?"

"Come into the kitchen and sit down," said Hamish soothingly. "I'm not mad. But I must tell you why I locked you up."

"I think you do owe me an explanation, but be quick about it!"

They sat at the kitchen table, and Hamish began. He told her all about the threats of Freddie Ionedes, and then he told her how Crystal had tried to lure him to his death.

When he finished, she looked half-angry, half-amused. "So you thought I was a hooker?"

The answer to that was "yes," but Hamish was not going to make matters worse.

"Look at it from my point of view," he said. "A beautiful woman such as yourself appears from nowhere and invites me to lunch. It all seemed so strange. I thought it was entrapment. I thought you were supposed to lure me somewhere where friends of Freddie could finish me off. I am so very sorry."

She looked at him suspiciously. "Is all this true?"

"Come into the office, and I'll get my official statement about the attempt on my life up on the computer."

She waited in the office until he found his statement, then he rose and said, "Sit down and read it. It's all there."

She read it very carefully, and then to his immeasurable relief, she smiled up at him. "You're forgiven."

"Can I make it up to you? The Falls of Anstey are very beautiful. I could run you up there."

"All right. Where's the bathroom? I need to repair my make-up."

When they left the police station together, they were faced not only by the residents but by Matthew, the local reporter, all snapping pictures.

"Get out of it!" shouted Hamish, but Tasman put a hand on his arm. "Smile," she said, "I'm used to it."

"Can we take your car?" asked Hamish. "I'm not really allowed to take civilians in the Land Rover unless I'm arresting them."

As she drove off, he asked, "What's it like to be so famous?"

"I take it as part of my job," she said. "I'm used to it. I'm making the most of it while I've still got my looks."

After inspecting the waterfall, they sat on a flat rock in the sun a little away from the noise of the tumbling water.

"Why did you never marry?" she asked. "You haven't been married, have you?"

Hamish found himself telling her all about Elspeth.

"But it seems to me," said Tasman, "that you had plenty of opportunities to ask her in the past. You shouldn't get married just for the sake of getting married."

"What about you?" asked Hamish.

"Maybe I will eventually if I meet someone. A lot of men like me as arm candy. I get to a lot of first nights and good restaurants." She put an arm round his shoulders. "Don't worry, Hamish. There's someone out there for both of us. Now, I'd better drop you back at the police station and then go to the hotel and pack."

"You're leaving! Why?"

"Because one of those photographs will appear in some newspaper. The local television stations will call on me, and then the nationals will chase me, hoping to catch me in an off moment."

✳   ✳   ✳

Later that day, the photo editor on the *Daily Bugle* approached Elspeth. "Don't you know that highland copper Hamish Macbeth?"

"Yes. Why?"

He slid a photo in front of her. "Good shot, eh?"

The photo showed Hamish in uniform, sitting on a rock with Tasman. She had her arm round his shoulders and was smiling into his eyes. "We thought we'd caption it, 'In the Arms of the Law.'"

"Very neat," said Elspeth with pretended indifference.

After he had gone, Elspeth felt miserable as all the memories of the fiasco of her wedding came flooding back. Luke had never come back to the newspaper. Nor had he written one word of apology. And here was Hamish Macbeth consorting with one of the world's most beautiful models. No one wanted her. She felt like crying.

The next day, Hamish angrily confronted Matthew Campbell in the local newspaper office. "Was that you who followed me and took that photograph?"

"It was, Hamish. Come on. It was very flattering. Think of all the men in Britain who would like to be in your shoes."

"She's packed up and left because of it. I feel like punching you."

"Don't. Did you ever hear what happened to Elspeth?"

"No. What? Is she married?"

"I was talking to someone at the *Bugle*, and he gave me the whole story."

Hamish listened to the humiliation of Elspeth. "Poor

lassie," he said. He thought of that sparkling ring locked in his safe. "Maybe I'll phone her."

But the days dragged on into high summer, and still he did not phone because he did not know quite what to say.

At the end of June, Hamish was on duty at the Highland Games in Braikie. The weather was fine, a rare treat for Braikie, because usually it poured with rain.

He wandered about, watching the events—the tossing the caber and swinging the hammer.

He bought himself an ice cream and was just considering strolling over to where the ferret racing was about to take place when he had an odd feeling of danger. He looked right and left. Fiona Fleming was there, walking on the arm of a wealthy-looking businessman. Mrs. Styles was selling jams and cakes at a church stall.

There was a police mobile unit set up to advise people on security. Sitting on the step was Pat Constable. She brightened when she saw him. "I was getting bored," she said. "No one seems to want to know about security."

"Want to come and watch the ferret racing?"

"I can't leave here. We never had that dinner. What about this evening?"

"There's a good Italian restaurant in Lochdubh," said Hamish. "I'll meet you there at eight. This event starts to close down at five o'clock. Have you seen anyone suspicious around? I keep getting a bad feeling."

"You're surely better at recognising strangers than me. This is your beat."

"I'll see you later."

Hamish walked off, trying to shake off the strange feeling of foreboding. He stopped at a stall set up by a gun shop in Dingwall. He recognised the owner, John Morrison. "Looking for a gun, Hamish?"

"Maybe. I wass thinking of a deer rifle." Hamish looked uneasily over his shoulder.

"What about this one?" John put a deer rifle on the counter. "This is a beauty. It's the Remington 700CDL. This is the newest, best-looking remodelling of the old standby Model 700. It's got a straight-comb American walnut stock with a satin finish, cut checkering, a right-hand cheekpiece, and a black fore-end tip and grip cap."

"Got any ammo?" asked Hamish.

"Of course."

"Load it up."

"Hamish, I just can't let you walk off with a loaded deer rifle."

"Chust for a wee minute," said Hamish. "I'll take it ower to that mobile unit. I want to show that policewoman."

"I suppose it's all right, you being the law and all." John deftly loaded it. "You shouldn't be carrying a loaded gun. Now, just over there and right back."

Hamish slung the gun over his shoulder, and then to John's horror, he ran off, zigzagging through the crowds. On and on pounded Hamish, up into the hills to where there was a ring of standing stones. He moved behind one of the stones and looked down the brae.

Three men came panting up through the heather. He saw the sun glinting off their weapons.

Borne on the wind came the tinny sounds of a carousel at the games.

Hamish raised the rifle to his shoulder and focussed. He took aim and fired. One man screamed, clutched his leg, and fell down. Bullets cracked against the standing stones. Hamish fired again and got another of the men in the arm. The third turned to flee. Hamish ran out from his hiding place and shouted, "Stop right there or you're dead."

The man stopped and dropped his gun. Hamish ran down to him and handcuffed him. He took out his phone and called for reinforcements. He cautioned the man he had handcuffed and then walked to each of the fallen men and cautioned them as well.

Three police officers who had been working at the games along with Pat Constable soon came running up the brae to join Hamish. He told them shortly that there had been an attempt on his life.

There was a long wait while ambulance men arrived with stretchers to take the two wounded men away. Then the one he had handcuffed was led off down to the road, where he was put into a police car.

Hamish's mobile rang. It was Jimmy Anderson. "I just heard the shout," he said. "What's been going on?"

"Three men came to kill me," said Hamish. "I think you'll find they had something to do with Freddie Ionedes. I've got something to wrap up here. I'll be over to Strathbane as soon as I can."

Hamish made his way quickly back to the games, fending off the excited questions from Pat Constable.

John Morrison came running to meet him. "Have you gone mad?"

"Look, John, I've got gun permits up to my ears. I felt I wass in danger. But I can hardly tell them I had a sixth sense that I was in danger."

John broke open the rifle, sniffed the barrel, and unloaded it. "You've fired it."

"Do this for me and I'll buy it," said Hamish, thinking miserably of his dwindling bank balance. "I'll come over to Dingwall soon and pick it up."

"They'll come down on me like a ton of bricks for having let you run off with a loaded rifle."

"I don't think they will. Not if you say what I'm going to tell you to say . . . Please?"

"Oh, all right."

"I want you to say that I was examining the deer rifle and you had just showed me how it loaded when I turned and saw the three men in the crowd. One of the men's jackets blew open, and I could see he had a gun. I guessed they had come for me. I wanted to avoid a shooting match in the middle of the games, and that is why I ran off."

"Where are you going now?"

"Strathbane."

"Before you go, a cheque or credit card would be welcome. That'll be five hundred and twenty-five pounds."

*   *   *

At police headquarters in Strathbane, Hamish was told that there would be a full enquiry into his shooting of the two men.

He groaned inwardly. Three gunmen had come after him, and yet he was the one who was to be investigated. He had endured a grilling from Daviot and had been told to wait for further questions.

He sat in the canteen and brooded over a cup of coffee, which tasted every bit as evil as the stuff he had at home.

He brightened up when Pat Constable came to join him. "I just heard you've got permission to go back to Lochdubh," she said. "But you're to report back here in the morning."

"I suppose our date's off," said Hamish.

"On the contrary. It's only seven o'clock. I'm off duty. Let's just go."

Hamish began to relax over the meal. Pat was cheerful, undemanding company. Occasionally one of the locals would approach their table, eager for details of the shooting, but Pat fended them off with, "Leave the man alone for now. He's had a bad shock."

"The fact is, I haven't," said Hamish. "It all seems like a dream now."

"You'll probably suffer from a wee bit of delayed shock tomorrow," said Pat. "Let's just go back to that nice police station of yours and go to bed."

Hamish could hardly believe his ears. "Oh, you mean, it's time I went to bed," he said cautiously.

She grinned cheekily. "No, I meant *we*. I'm propositioning

you, Hamish Macbeth. We're both single, and we've both had a hard day. We deserve some fun."

"Just like that!"

"Why not?"

"I don't have . . . er . . . and Patel's is closed."

"I have. Come into the twenty-first century, Hamish. Women don't wait around to be asked any more."

Back at the police station, while Pat used the bathroom, Hamish went into the police office. He looked thoughtfully at his answering machine. Then he unplugged it. He was not going to risk either Priscilla or Elspeth phoning him and spoiling things. Would it all be as casual as it seemed? Or would she expect some sort of commitment?

The hell with it, he thought. He had been celibate long enough.

Freddie Ionedes sat on the bed in his cell and looked up at his lawyer, Simon Devize, otherwise known behind his back as Sleazy Simon.

"I want that Macbeth dead," he said. "Tell Brandon."

Brandon was his second in command.

"Brandon is going to point out that six of our people are already in the slammer thanks to your vendetta," said Simon.

"He'll do as he's told," growled Freddie. "Get on with it."

Simon left the prison and got into his car and drove off. In his rear-view mirror, he saw a black BMW following him. When he considered he was safely clear of the prison, he stopped and got out. The BMW stopped behind him.

Simon went up to it. The passenger window lowered, and Brandon stared at him. "Well?"

"His orders are you're to go after that highland policeman again."

"He's mad. Look, I'm in charge now. Tell him okay on your next visit. Keep him happy. He'll die in prison. Someone's got to run the show. But between ourselves, I'm not going to lose any more men. Got it?"

"I've got it."

Hamish slowly came awake. He felt a warm body next to his own and smiled sleepily, turned over, and threw an arm around his cat.

"What the hell!" He sat up in bed. The animals had been banished from the bedroom the night before.

There was a note on the pillow next to his own. He read, "Got to go on duty. See you later. Thanks for a great night. Love, Pat."

Could it be as easy as that? he wondered. No demands to see him again. No waiting around until he woke to make him breakfast.

He stretched and yawned, looked at the clock, and let out a yelp of horror. It was ten o'clock in the morning.

He had a hurried shower and shave and put on his uniform and had just finished when the kitchen door opened and Jimmy Anderson strolled in.

"Are they screaming for me?" asked Hamish.

"No, they're too thrilled with the men you captured. They're singing like canaries. Oh, what's this note on the table? It says,

'Got you some decent coffee. Love and kisses, Pat.' Well, well, well. Would that be Pat Constable?"

Hamish flushed angrily and snatched the note. "No, Pat is a frisky old lady in the village that sometimes gives me wee presents."

"I should have known you wouldn't be that lucky. Scotland Yard's coming up again. Blair is ferreting around to see if he can take the credit for something."

"How are the two I shot?"

"They'll live. One clean shot through the arm on one, and one shot in the hip on the other. Blair tried to tell Daviot you were lucky. I pointed out you'd won shooting prizes all over the Highlands."

"I hope it's over and Freddie won't send any more goons after me."

"With all the information pouring out of the three, I think Freddie's going to find his empire is being wound up in a few weeks' time. I don't think you've anything to worry about."

"I'd better get over to headquarters," said Hamish.

"Take your time. Everyone's trying to get a bit of the action and keep you out of it."

Hamish followed Jimmy's car over to Strathbane. All he could think of was seeing Pat again.

But as he drifted around the building that day, waiting to be interviewed again, he could not see her. By early evening, he was sitting in the canteen again, deciding to ask for permission to go home, when Pat suddenly appeared. She gave him a kiss on the cheek. "How are you, lover boy?"

"Great. Just about to ask permission to leave. No one seems to want to ask me any questions. I suppose I'd better enjoy it because when the enquiry comes along, I'll have to suffer hours of questioning. Are you off duty?"

"Just finished."

"What about coming back with me?"

"Can't, Hamish. I'm nipping down to Inverness to see my boyfriend."

Hamish looked at her in amazement. "Your boyfriend. Is it serious?"

"We'll probably get engaged. We've been looking at a few houses."

"Pat Constable, you are not only immoral but amoral."

She threw him that cheeky grin of hers. "Grand, isn't it?" She gave him a smacking kiss on the mouth and trotted off.

Epilogue

They sin who tell us love can die,
With life all other passions fly,
All others are but vanity.

—Robert Southey

Court cases over, evidence given, and a late spring smiling on the Highlands made Hamish feel that the bad days were over.

On one of his days off, he was lying in a deckchair in his front garden with his animals at his feet. Sometimes he thought of Elspeth and sometimes of Priscilla, but each time he banished the thoughts as quickly as possible. He would settle for being a bachelor. He had even refused an invitation to dinner from that pretty policewoman, Pat Constable.

When Mary Gannon's face loomed over the garden hedge, he felt a stab of irritation at having his lazy day interrupted.

He got to his feet. "Come round to the kitchen door and don't lecture me. It's my day off."

When Mary entered the kitchen, she said placatingly, "It's

my day off as well. I thought I'd see how you were getting on."

"Fine. What about you?"

"Not bad. I'm enjoying being in Inverness now. Not so many chauvinist pigs around."

"Tea? Coffee?"

"Tea, please. Do you always keep that stove on? It's warm today."

"I haven't had a bath yet, and the back boiler heats the water. Saves a fortune on electricity bills. Did you see my new Land Rover? I'm right proud of it."

"Very fine."

"You know," said Hamish, lifting down the teapot from a cupboard, "I still feel silly being tricked by Gloria. How was I to know she'd slip Rohypnol in my drink?"

"Look at it this way," said Mary. "It was the last thing you would expect to happen to you in the north of snowbound Scotland. No one would have believed that Freddie Ionedes would dare to show his face anywhere in the country. All that rubbish about we look after our own. Probably Crystal told him if he didn't finish you off, she'd talk about that other murder. As it was, of course she did. Imagine! A Labour MP, Mr. Sorley, man of the people, frequenting an expensive knocking shop like that? His wife was shattered."

"She didnae get a chance to tell the paper she was standing by her man," said Hamish cynically. "They aye do that."

"She's not too badly off. She's married again. What about you? Still single?"

"Aye, and determined to stay that way."

"Did that reporter get married?"

"I don't know."

Hamish filled the teapot and put mugs, sugar, and milk on the table.

"I could find out for you."

"Let it be."

"You know, I often wonder about that packet Mrs. Gillespie left for Mrs. Samson. I suppose we'll never know what became of it now."

In his bedroom in a suburb of Toronto, Robert Macgregor, a lanky teenager, was clearing out his room. His father had said he'd take his belt to him if the mess hadn't been cleared up by the time he got home.

Robert stacked old magazines and posters into rubbish bags. He fished under the bed and took out a supply of pornographic magazines to get rid of before his father arrived for the evening inspection.

He opened one of them for a last look, and a packet fell out on the floor. He picked it up. He'd need to get rid of it. He remembered that last year he had been sent down to the mailbox to collect the mail. There had only been this packet. He had tripped on the road back up the drive, and the packet had fallen in a puddle. Terrified of getting into a row, he had shoved the packet up under his sweater and then had shoved it inside that magazine under his bed.

From the address on the back, he knew it was from his great-aunt in Scotland, Flora Samson. He opened it up to see if there was any money in it, but it was only letters and a few photographs. There was a letter in spidery writing. It said, "My dear niece, I want you to keep this safe for me and post it back to me when I tell you to. Your loving aunt, Flora."

He stuffed it into one of the rubbish bags. He remembered his mother had gone over for the funeral. His great-aunt was dead now, so it was probably not important anyway.